She Broke Up, I Didn't!
. . . I Just Kissed Someone Else!

Other Books by Durjoy Datta

Of Course I Love You..!
Now That You're Rich!
Ohh Yes, I Am Single!
You Were My Crush!
If It's Not Forever!

She Broke Up, I Didn't!

. . . I Just Kissed Someone Else!

Durjoy Datta

GRAPEVINE INDIA

Grapevine India Publishers Pvt. Ltd.

Plot no.4, First Floor

Pandav Nagar,

Opposite Shadipur Metro Station,

Patel Nagar,

New Delhi - 110008

India

grapevineindiapublishers@gmail.com

contact@grapevineindia.in

First published by Grapevine India Publishers in 2011

Copyright © Durjoy Datta, 2010

Typeset and layout design: A & D. Co.

*To the girl who had vodka bottles stashed
under her bed*

Acknowledgements

Amazing things have happened since August 2008, the month when '*Of Course I Love You! . . . Till I Find Someone Better*' saw the light of the day. And still more amazing things followed after the release of '*Now That You're Rich . . . Let's fall In love!*' in August 2009. Though I would like to thank like a million people for everything that I have seen in the past three years that I have been writing, but since it would be immensely boring for you, I would keep the list short and sweet.

Many people whom I thank below have unwaveringly stood beside me while I finished this manuscript in record time, guiding me, criticizing me and supporting me. I hope their efforts pay off. I thank Maanvi Ahuja, for always being there, no matter how stupidly or senselessly I have acted.

Sachin Garg for letting me know every day that I can kick some serious ass this time, Ekta Mehta for being so unrealistically sweet, supportive . . . and beyond awesome! Vaaruni Dhawan for being such an incredibly cute influence in my life, Neeti Rustagi for being with me all these years, Savvy Singh for the helping hand she has always extended, Rohini Khanna for fooling me into believing that I am worth something, Surabhi Guha Mazumdar for being the awesome person she is, Uttara Rao for being such a boost to my ego, Hansita for the one who bears the brunt of my typos the most, Chhavi Kharuna for all the spiritual *gyaan*, Ankita Mehta for just being there!

I also thank these people for making my life as good as it is right now—Nikita Singh, Naman Kapur, Abhishek Sachdev, Nitin Verma, Aeshna Nigam, Vandana Vidyarthi, Anupriya Aggarwal, Ekta Bharadwaj, Geetika Maheshwari, Geetika Saxena, Varun, Neha Kakkar, Soumi Das, Shreyasi Bose, Medha Shree, Nidhi Sharma, Gunjan Sayal, Rumpa Roy Chauhan,

Neha Kakkar, Gunjan Upreti.

Arpit Khandelwal, Ankit Mittal, Abhishek Chopra, Ashish Rander, Eeshaan Sharma, Tigmanshu Dubey, Mukul Gupta for making college life at MDI what it should be like—Awesome! I thank the entire batches of MDI PG 08 and 09, especially PG09 Section—C, simply because I love these guys.

Now to thank people who really matter—My extended family for they have always been there. And Guruji, because without his blessings all this would still have been a distant dream!

Flashbacks of a Fool—ME!

The days were long. Long as they had never been. The air was still in the room. Nothing moved. It had been three days since I had moved out of that room. It had been three days since I had broken up with Avantika. I read a page from my old diary from three years back, where I used to recount every important day of my life. The first time I had met Avantika was one of them.

There were people in that incident who were no longer in my life. Tanmay—Avantika's brother, Vernita—My best friend, three years back. They were not a part of my life now. Not anymore.

Avantika was. She will always be. I guess . . .

September 2007.

Today was a day when I spent most of my time with my eyes and mouth wide open. Tanmay's sister had just landed and lately Vernita and she had become bitching partners.

'I just have to drop an assignment, Deb,' Vernita said as she tagged me along to see her guy, Tanmay.

'Assignments? I thought all your assignments are done at his place,' I said, taking a dig at her malleable morals. She was pretty bugged with my constant jibes on her malleable morals by the time we reached Greater Kailash.

We met Tanmay outside his uncle's house. Good looks ran in the family, Tanmay was one of the better looking guys, that made guys who look like me, seem like douche bags.

'She is coming in a moment. And she is looking forward to meet you,' Tanmay said, after Vernita asked where his sister was.

'Who? Me?' I was taken by surprise.

'Yeah,' he said.

'And why is that?'

'I told her that you were this awesome guy who could hook up with any girl,' Tanmay said.

Such descriptions do nothing other than ensure failure . . . and looking forward sounded more like I-will-see-him. And I was not awesome! Lucky with opposite sex? Yes. Awesome guy? No!

Avantika had been to a rehab for her drugs and alcohol problem but that was more than a year back. I had already started imagining Avantika as a leather-jacketed gothic chic with metal piercing on every visible and non-visible part of her body, not to forget the black nail polish.

'Here she comes,' Vernita said.

That could have been the last thing I remembered from that day had I had a weak heart. I had passed out for a few seconds for sure. I skipped a beat or maybe it had just stopped beating altogether. I was choking. There was a strange churning in my bowels. I felt the blood rush down to the ends of my arteries and then burst out. I could feel my brain imploding. I was going to die and I was sure.

She was breathtakingly beautiful . . . I guess unrealistically beautiful is more like it! All the things that I used to say to sleep with my ex-girlfriends had just come true. She was a dream. Even better, you could not even dream of something so perfect. Plastic surgeons still cannot rival God, I thought.

She was so hard to describe. Those limpid constantly wet black eyes screamed for love. There is nothing better than a melancholic beautiful face. The moonlight reflected off her perfectly sculpted face, seemed the only light illuminating the place. Somebody stood with a blower nearby to get her streaked hair to cover her face so that she could look sexier flicking it away from her eyes. She had those big eyes of a month old child, big and screaming for attention, a perfectly drafted nose, flawless bright pink lips and a creamy white complexion that would put Photoshop to shame. Oh hell, she was way out of my league. She was a goddamn goddess or she was the devil. She could not possibly be human.

I just could not look beyond her face. It was strange, as it had never happened that way. Things were generally the other way around. Cup size did not make the first impression this time.

'Hi Vernita! How are you?' She said.

Her voice was music to my ears. It tingled . . . I can still hear it in my head, over and over again.

They hugged. Avantika had turned out in a simple dull brown kurta and jeans, without even a hint of make-up. She with all her simplicity was far in contrast to how Vernita had described her to me as. Even though I am an ardent fan of short skimpy skirts and deep necklines, I loved what she was wearing or maybe it wasn't about the clothes anymore.

I was not seeing right, I was not hearing right. I was just lost in the reflecting pools in those beautiful eyes. My heart pounded so hard it felt like it would pop out of my chest any moment.

'Hi! How are you Debashish?' She serenaded with a big golden harp as I spotted her with a halo and two big white wings fluttering behind her, somewhere up in the clouds. Drugs? Alcohol? Leather? She would not even know all that. I did see the remnants of a piercing just above her left eyebrow, and sure enough, a tattoo peeked out from her sleeve: a red swastik sign.

Okay, relax, it is just a dream. It will be over in a while, I told myself.

'Are you okay?' she asked.

'I am okay,' I said in what seemed like my fourth attempt at speaking after the first three ended in soundless flapping of my tongue. It was a strange feeling—I was nervous, shit nervous. I felt small. I felt ugly. I felt insignificant. Was I fine? I guess she wasn't aware that half of the people she met probably either slipped into a coma or ended up thinking that the meeting never happened, believing that it was just a figment of their imagination. I was lucky I was breathing.

'You guys talk, we will just take a walk,' Tanmay said as he and Vernita turned away from us.

I looked at her and smiled stupidly. I wondered if her dog looked cuter than I did.

'They look good. Don't they?'

They looked like peasants before her.

'Yes,' I said. I was trying not to stare into those fall-in-love-with-me eyes.

'I didn't quite like Vernita when I first met her. I kind of like her now. She is a little too brash, isn't she?'

'Yes.' I like your nose, can I touch it?

'What do you think? Are they serious for each other?'

'Yes.' I like your lips, are they for real?

'You don't talk much, do you?'

'Yes.' I like your eyes, do they ever close?

Was she kidding? Was I not trying? I could have said a million things, mostly stupid, but my senses had still not recovered from the shock her overwhelmingly good looks that I had just been subjected to, had given me. I was trying hard not to make eye contact and stay in my senses and there she was, mocking me for my dumbness.

'And why are you constantly looking down? I hope I am not that ugly?'

It was strange that she asked me that because I truly had not seen someone who was so perfect in its existence that you feel humbled. The simplicity of what she came wearing, the honesty in her smile, the serenading voice, the depth of her eyes— unforgettable.

It's moments like these that you wait for not knowing what you are waiting for, but when they come . . . you know that this is something you could have waited your whole life for.

It has been four hours since I took her leave but I cannot get her out of my head. That smile, those eyes . . . they are just not leaving me. As I sleep today, I wish to see her again. Soon.

~

This was the day that marked the end of my reckless dating days, when the only consideration while choosing a girl used to be whether she would sleep with me within a week or not! That day I really felt something tugged more inside my shirt than something did lower down.

It had been three and half years since then, and I had fallen in love with this girl every single day of the twelve hundred and seventy five days that we had been together. I have been more in love with her every new day than the day before.

Between that day and today, she has only got more beautiful, more charming, more adorable and lovelier. Why *me*, of all the guys she could land? I had never managed to figure that one out!

Quintessential Avantika

I had been tense for the last few days. Interviews for summer internships had started. Avantika and I did not want to go to different cities for our internships.

'I am sure I will screw this one up,' I said as my palms started sweating. The company had shortlisted fifteen students for interviews. They had planned to take just four. Avantika and I were the last few in the preference order that the company had stated.

'You will not,' she said and rubbed my hands.

'But why if they take the first four guys and leave the campus? We might not even get a chance for an interview!' I said.

Many companies did that. They did not want to interview a whole lot of people to choose their interns. They specified an order in which the students should come. If they like the person, they would take him and close the placement process. The students lower down in the interview schedule might not even get a chance!

'Let's hope for the best!' she said.

'Avantika? Rubbing you hand like that on my shoulder

would only distract me,' I said.

'You clear the interview and I would do it without your clothes on,' she winked.

'I won't get through.'

'You will. Trust me,' she said.

When two beautiful eyes lined with kohl look at you and say that with conviction, you cannot help but believe it. She smiled at me and it calmed my nerves a little.

The first interview was over! The guy came out smiling and with an offer letter in hand. My hopes died. There were just three more seats to fill up and there were ten interviews before me. There was no way Avantika and I were clearing this interview together.

'Now what!' I said.

'. . . chill, Deb. There are still three seats left.'

'And ten guys to interview! What if they even choose two?'

'Hmm,' she said. For the first time that morning, I saw her a little tense. 'I should go talk to the guy handling this thing.'

'What can *he* change?' I asked irritably.

'Let's see,' she said and handed over her file to me.

Avantika looked stunning that day. She seemed to have jumped out of a female formal wear fashion magazine: a well-rounded ass that made the short skirt she wore look fabulous, a perfect fitted blazer and shiny black pointed stilettos completed the picture. She made the clothes look good and not vice versa. There were whispers in the corridors in our college that morning, *'Obviously, she will get through! She is so hot!'*

Anyway, Avantika got up and walked up to the college representative who handled everything. There were hushed whispers around me. I saw Avantika flash the best of her smiles in front of the college senior, the representative.

What is she doing?

I heard the guy sitting next to me tell his friend. I did not feel too good about what was happening. Avantika talked to that senior for a little while, came back, and sat next to me.

'What was going on there?' I asked.

'Nothing. Just be prepared. You will be the next one to be interviewed. Do well,' she pulled up my tie.

What!

The guy from the interview room came out. He was not selected.

'Debashish Roy, you're next', the college representative said.

I got up and entered the room. The whispers of other shortlisted students grew louder. They knew what had happened. Yet, another guy had fallen to the charms of Avantika. Avantika had always been intimidating for people who did not know her. One stern statement from her and the authority crushes you. One smile of hers and you are charmed, lost in those beautiful sparkling eyes and the dazzling smile. It had been three years and I was still trying to cope with these.

Anyway, the interview was slightly long, but I had been taught well by Avantika. Soon, they slipped the offer letter in front of me. I signed the document and came out smiling. People saw me with disgust. *Used his girlfriend to get through*, they muttered under their breath. *Fuck you*, I muttered under my.

I sat there with Avantika and hoped no one else made it. The next few went in for the interview and no one got it. *Eat that motherfucker*, I said in my head every time someone left that room without an offer.

Finally, they called Avantika in. There were still two seats left. And as expected, she kicked ass!

'To my room,' she said, even before I could congratulate her.

Twenty minutes later, we were in her hostel room, naked. Our well-ironed suits lay crumpled and strewn across the floor. Our bodies were a tangled heap of flesh. We could not tell where I ended and she started, with our legs and hands interlocked around each other. She was still wearing her stilettos. My socks had still not left my feet.

'That was good,' she said.

'Good? That was awesome.'

'Yeah. You were good. I was the awesome,' she winked.

I was still tired and panting from the session, when I saw a few tears in her eyes.

'Aw! What happened baby?' I asked her.

'. . . am I a slut?'

'You? *Why?*' I asked.

I knew what she hinted at. The college would talk about what happened today. Avantika had flirted with a college senior to tamper with the interview order. Had she not changed it, I may have not cracked it. *Slut*, I knew people would call her that.

'You're mine, baby,' I said.

'Hmm, anyway, they don't matter. We do,' she said and wiped off her tears.

'Just curious—what did you say to him?'

'I just requested him that since you have no other shortlists, that you should be allowed in first. That this was your last chance at a decent internship . . .'

'Didn't he know that I had three more shortlists?'

'. . . I guess he forgot,' she winked.

We kissed.

I was happy that we had got through the same company but . . . I did not like that she had to flirt with someone to get it done. People talked about it a few days and then forgot. It hurt her when people said things to her behind her back, but she tried not to show it.

Assholes.

Didn't I Just Love Her?

'**H**ey!' I waved my hand from the lift itself.

She looked and ignored my frantic hand movements across the hallway, went back to the computer screen. I walked slowly through the cubicles on both sides, and smiled at people who knew me and they smiled back at me. Most of them knew where I was heading to. *Everyone* did.

'Good morning,' I said as her perfume wafted inside my nostrils. The perfume was my third anniversary gift and she had vowed to wear it every single day. She had made the fragrance as her own. Three days in a swampy tent in Ooty and she would still smell the same. Naked or with clothes on, going to sleep or getting up, after a shower or before one, she still would smell *awesome*.

'What *the* hell were you doing there?' she asked angrily as she looked at me.

She didn't know that her frowning eyebrows and the wide open eyes didn't scare anyone. It just made her look more adorable. It's as cute as a puppy being angry at the rubber ball. *That* cute!

'I was just excited to see you.'

She turned away from me and flicked her hair behind her ear, 'You don't have to show the entire floor that you were excited.'

'What? Everyone knows that we are together,' I said as I looked at her.

She had gotten fairer, if that was possible. Her nose looked a little red from the chill in the air; her lips a more little red and cheeks a little more pull-able.

She looked fabulous.

'Not the bosses. They don't know about *us*.'

'So what? What if they know?' I asked, as I pulled up a chair from the nearby desk.

'They are old people Deb, they don't understand all this.'

'What all this?' I teased her.

'. . . that I am seeing you and we are in love!' she said, her eye lashes flapped over those big almond shaped eyes.

'*Love*? Let me get this thing totally clear with you Avantika. I just *lust* for you, nothing more, and nothing less.'

'Oh . . . Mr Deb just *lusts* me?' She looked at me, her big brown eyes on me. 'Is it so?'

'It sure is,' I said.

'Then you really don't mind,' she turned away from me and tapped on the keyboard, 'if I check out other guys' profiles on Facebook . . . Oh, I think *this* one is hot. Should I send him a friend request? He would be hot in bed too, I guess. But why look outside, when I have *Kabir* here?'

My heart shrunk. Though I knew she was just playing around, it still hurt. It didn't help that Kabir was taller, fairer and better accomplished. Kabir always had the hots for my girlfriend like every guy with a working organ had.

'Why . . . w . . . why would I mind? Go ahead . . . sleep with him . . . I don't mind. Did I tell you? Last night was awesome. Malini is incredible in bed. I mean, she is really good.'

Avantika looked at me, her eyes quivering and still big, '*Never* say that.'

Avantika and I had been going out since three years now, and except for one break-up that lasted a little while, it had been a smooth ride. Well, not *really*. The days were smooth, the nights—*rough*. I wasn't complaining. Three years and empty classrooms, hostel rooms, secluded roads and movie hall: things like these still *excited* us.

We still couldn't keep our hands off each other. I used to feel like making out with her all the time. Why she felt the same? I never found out the reason for that. Maybe she just pitied how ugly I was. Otherwise, a girl like *her* had no business to even kiss a guy a like me.

'So, season eight?' she asked.

'Whichever would do.'

'The Man with The Long Stick?' she asked.

'No, that is a little boring.'

'The Turkey?'

'No, that, we have seen a million times.'

'The Gas Burst?'

'Umm . . . no,' I shook my head. 'Why don't we watch the fifth season, the third or the fourth episode?'

'Why don't you say it in the first place?' she said, a little miffed.

'I like it when you ask.'

'*Bullshit.*'

She hit the play button. It was probably the hundredth time we were watching this episode, but I didn't mind. Every time, it was funnier than the last time. I had tried watching those sitcoms alone, but they are never as much fun as they are with her.

She walked and snuggled up to me, passed on the popcorn and closed her eyes. 'What do you think will happen tomorrow?' she asked.

'You will get it, that's what,' I said.

'Are you sure?'

'Yes.'

'Hmm . . .' she felt a bit relaxed and hugged me tighter.

The next day was pretty exciting for interns like her who were expecting a pre-placement offer. Oh, I didn't tell you about *that.* Avantika and I were dating since our college days in Delhi. It was an awesome time for both of us. We were young and we did pretty *silly* stuff back then. Not that we don't do that anymore, but that time was great.

After we both passed out from our colleges, we joined the same firm in Hyderabad. Things were going perfect for us. We were just twenty two but had started planning our future together. On days when we were sure that we would always be together, she even told me what names she had decided for her kids. We were *that* serious. It seemed like nothing could separate us.

It had been a while that we had been working when recession hit our firm and I was thrown out of the company. I worked for a smaller firm for a couple of months but it wasn't really the same. That is when we decided we needed to study further.

And like everyone, we thought we should do our MBA too.

Both of us joined coaching institutes. We studied hard for a couple of months.

'*No touching me, until we study for three hours.*' This was her mantra to make me study. It helped. We cleared a few exams. Or rather, *she* did—IIM-Indore, IIM- Kolkata, FMS, and MDI. Unlike her, I didn't have a choice. I had just cleared MDI, Gurgaon.

I wanted her to take the right decision and join the college that was best for her career. However, she always found out something that would swing the balance in favour of MDI, Gurgaon! Naah, I lied there. I never wanted her to take the *right* decision and go to IIM Kolkata! I played my part in getting her to join MDI.

The first year was total breeze there. We had nothing to do with whatever happened in college. Yes, once in a while, a guy used to walk up to her and ask her to participate in one of the numerous fests in college, but we had *nothing* to do with them.

I was glad it was that way. She and I. We needed no one else.

It was the last day of our internship. I couldn't wait to go back to college. It had been two months that I had been going to that office in suffocating formals and I couldn't take it anymore.

The managers called all of us on our last working day, the interns, and gave us an extensive review on how each one of us did during the internship. The reviews for Avantika and Kabir stood out. I slept through most of it. I just wanted to hear whether they would offer Avantika a job or not! That's all I cared for. The conference ended and we all moved out.

We had all expected that they would announce the names

of the interns they had chosen for a job but they didn't. They said they needed more time to decide since everyone was so brilliant. Obviously, they weren't talking about *me*.

'What do you think of the chances?' she asked me cutely.

'You will get through! Did you not hear what he said? You were brilliant, and I didn't hear him say these words for anyone else.

'You are just being sweet,' she said.

'Why would be I be sweet?'

'Because you know that, since we have the rest of the day free, we can do a lot of things that are more than sweet,' she looked at me with her seductive *undress-me* eyes.

I wanted to take her back to the conference room and tell her that she had not been brilliant. I longed to tell her that she had been *dirty* and punish her for it. I wanted to make her pay. But then, Avantika had *other* ideas. She wanted to go to the Human Resources department to check if the internship stipends were ready. The guy sitting there said that the money was already transferred into our accounts that morning. Avantika smiled. I didn't. My mind was still in the conference room.

'What do we do now?' she asked.

'Two options. We can go back to our place and do something *very* interesting,' I paused.

'I will take the second one,' she said.

'Or we can go to your place and do something interesting.'

'Deb, I am serious!'

'What? I don't know! You decide.' *Can we make out? In the conference room?*

'You are the guy! You should decide these things,' she said.

'I have an *idea*,' I said and looked at her.

My eyes must have given away what was on my mind.

Avantika rarely let me down.

A little later, I found myself following her into the conference room. The people in the cubicles who looked at us as we walked past them had no idea what was on our minds.

We bolted the door behind us. The projector of the room was still running. Avantika killed the other lights. We were alone in that room. She unbuttoned the first of her many buttons and looked at me. Her long legs shifted in their place as she waited for me to behave savagely with her. She expected no mercy from me. It was time to *punish* her. She looked ready and I couldn't wait any longer. We were scared, but the thrill of making out in an office conference room couldn't have been ignored.

We made out. The conference room was soundproof. We checked it well. She had shouted and screamed out my name! And so had I. Three years, and we still made out like it was our first time.

As we lay on the floor of the conference room, exhausted, she said, 'Let's go away, Deb.'

After every heavenly make-out, Avantika used to say something very romantic. This time was no different.

'Go away? Where?'

'Anywhere? Somewhere far from here. There are still five days to go for college and we have nothing to do.'

'We can just stay at my place and do *nothing*.'

'That's boring,' she said, 'Let's go to Goa? It's not that far!'

'Are you serious?' I asked her. I had always wanted to see her in a bikini. Maybe, it wasn't a bad idea after all.

'I am,' she said and rested her head on my shoulder.

'Goa it is!'

We smiled at each other. Soon, we realised that we couldn't

lay around naked in the conference room much longer. We got up, checked each other's necks for love bites, kissed each other one more time and headed back to our seats.

There had never been a dull day in the last three years. Avantika and I *were* the perfect couple. Even in the darkest of the times, which I can safely say weren't many, weren't dark enough for us. At least for me, one look at her usually solved every problem.

Well, maybe sometimes more than a look. Like that day, a *quickie* in the conference room solved everything.

I had been really excited about the Goa plan, but packing is such a pain. I got irritated in a while and called her up. Well, actually I hadn't even started to pack. I had my clothes strewn all over the bed, the dining table, the washroom . . . they were everywhere! I didn't know where to start.

Avantika had already packed and was on her way to my place! I panicked, grabbed hold of all the clothes and stuffed them inside two suitcases. There were still boxers, socks, trousers and million other things strewn all across the house. I gave up. It was a lost cause.

'How much more time will you need to pack, Deb?' she asked as the cab driver piled up five of her seven suitcases neatly over one another in the drawing room.

'Avantika? *Exactly* how many clothes do you have?'

'Leave that,' she said and paid the cab driver. She was yet to look around.

What? Yes, she was shocked for a little while. My flat looked like a rat hole where the rats had died. It was dirty and it stank. That's why I loved Avantika so much. Despite everything, she loved me! I mean, *how?* Even I didn't love myself.

'What the hell is this Deb? Your flat is a mess,' she shrieked and immediately rolled up her sleeves.

'You don't have to bother with that. Let's just pack and leave,' I said.

It was already too late. She was a cleanliness freak. A speck of dust and she would rush to clean it. One soiled pair of boxers in one corner of the room, and she would make it her agenda to get my whole wardrobe washed. The only reason why my room in the MDI hostel was probably *the* cleanest of all rooms, including the girls' rooms and excluding hers, was Avantika! My roommate was happy that I was dating her. *'Deb, I will pay you, but please don't break up with her!'* he used to say.

'Deb, is this how you pack?' She yanked open the suitcases and the clothes spilled over. It was like the suitcase threw up. 'And you have mixed all your stuff. These are so smelly. And don't just sit around there. Come and help me with this.'

I went there and pretended to do something. I had *no* idea what to do!

'You are doing nothing, Deb. Just go and do whatever you want to do,' she said angrily.

I couldn't have turned her down. So, I just sat there and looked at her as she neatly segregated the clothes and then placed them in different bags and suitcases.

She looked beautiful. It had been three years and I was yet to stop marvelling at how great she looked. As the rays from the window reflected off her flawless complexion, I felt guilty as a man. I should have been trying to get her naked and not stare at her, as if it was the first time I had seen her. I didn't deserve her. I had just got *lucky*.

She bent over and started to close the suitcases. I could spot a love bite from the morning. I smiled and said to myself, '*I did that.*'

'I am done,' she said.

The bags and suitcases were done. And I had never seen my apartment so clean. It almost sparkled!

'So, we leave now?' I asked.

'In a while,' she said. 'Let me catch some breath first.' She flopped down beside me.

'Care for mouth to mouth respiration?'

'Shit, Deb . . . Have you even brushed today?'

'I have!'

'You still smell like shit,' she laughed.

'Why don't you simply say you don't want to kiss me?'

'Didn't I do that just this morning?' she said.

She pulled me by the collar and planted a long one on my lips. And as it happened every time, bolts of electricity ran through my spine as she pulled me deeper inside her mouth. Her sweet lips and rampaging tongue turned my world upside down *every* time they touched mine. She let me go while she still stared in my eyes.

'You actually taste like shit,' she winked.

'But you seem to like it.'

'I love it,' she said and pecked me.

Now how many girls can claim to give their guys an erection with a peck after three years in a relationship? Not to forget that we had just made out in the morning! Avantika could.

She knew that . . . and must have felt it sometime or the other!

The plan to Goa was cancelled, like every other plan. There was never a better plan than just being in her arms. She told me that she was tired and I told her that we should just hug each other, sleep and take rest. Avantika nodded like a little child and buried her head inside my chest.

'So we are not going anywhere then, are we?' she asked, her eyes twinkling.

'Does it look like we are going?'

'Are we just sleeping?' she asked.

'Yes,' I said and made her lie down on a pillow.

'Where are you going? I need someone to hug,' she said and my heart melted in unrecognizable blobs.

'I will just come.'

'Okay,' she said, rubbed her face on the pillow, closed her eyes and smiled.

I took a mental note—Burn the pillow, she loves it! I returned with my internship stipend in hand.

'Come here,' she said and pulled me inside the quilt, 'and go nowhere,' she said and kissed me.

'I am not going anywhere,' I kissed her back. 'I have something for you.'

'I want it if it is a long hug.'

'That too,' I said and fished it out of my pocket. '*This* is for you.'

'What is . . . ?' she paused, 'Oh . . . this is beautiful, this is so beautiful!' she said as she took the ring in her hand. She immediately got up and stared at it. Light reflected from all the lines and cuts of the stones in the ring.

'Thank you so much, baby! Won't you help me wear it?' she asked.

I slipped in it her finger.

'I didn't know you had a taste in junk jewellery,' she said.

Have you ever been kicked in your nuts? If you are a girl, then obviously, you know how it is like. You go through those *difficult* three days every month. I felt exactly like that. I just learnt that I had spent two months of my hard earned money on a ring that looked like it had been picked off the street. Junk jewellery? Was my choice *that* bad?

'Deb?' she said as I stared blankly at the ring. *Why?* It looked all right. Even the over eager sales girl said I had a brilliant choice and that my girl would be very happy. Liar, I thought.

'This is real,' I said.

'Real, as in?' she asked, a little puzzled.

'This is in real gold baby, and these are real stones. I got it from Tiffany's,' I said, a little dejected.

'Don't tell me. This . . .' she looked surprised. 'It is *really* nice.'

'You don't have to lie now. You just said it. Never mind, it is for you. You can get it changed if you want to,' I said, trying not to sound low. I wondered if I had kept the bill or thrown it away. Forty thousand rupees worth of junk. *Fuck my life.*

'Three years and you still don't know anything about me!' she smiled.

'What?'

'I could tell you how many grams this weighs, and its item code, for heavens' sake! A girl knows a *real* diamond amongst a heap of glass pieces!'

'Huh?'

'The minute I saw it, I knew it was real!'

'You bitch!'

'And thank you so much!' She hugged me and kissed me. 'This is beautiful! And pretty expensive too!'

'You don't have to worry about that.'

'I have to. I don't want to marry a guy with no bank balance!'

'Marry? How many times do I have to say it is just *lust*?'

She snuggled up to me and whispered, 'If it is just lust, then why don't you just take all my clothes off and *fuck* me?'

'I would rather just see you sleep.'

'Good boy,' she said, closed her eyes and rested her head in my arms. 'You smell nice.'

Just see you sleep? Did I just say that? I asked her to go to sleep when she had just asked me to *fuck* her? I *hated* myself. That's what happens when you're in love. You are offered sex and you turn it down because you think that the person looks amazingly cute when she is sleeping. Horrible.

Of When We Went to Pune . . .
and Goa

It was late evening when we woke up amidst the packed suitcases and nowhere to go.

'What do you want to do for the next three days, baby?' I asked her as I kissed her on the forehead.

'Don't disturb me, let me finish the dream,' she said and turned away from me.

'It's not a dream if you are awake,' I said and she punched me.

I waited for five minutes, while I could see her closed eyes quivering and her lips curving into a small smile.

'What was the dream all about?'

'Nothing much, the usual,' she said.

'Either you don't tell me such things or if you do, complete them! Tell me what the dream was about?'

'Umm . . . we were . . . you know . . . kind of getting married.'

It was kind of strange to hear such things from her. Why would she even consider being married to me! I was just another one of the million guys who had the hots for her. If I were to list down all the guys who had a crush on her, or had asked her out, I don't think even all the toilet papers in the world can give me the requisite space. The list is *that* long!

'So where was the wedding?' I asked.

'I don't know.'

'Who all were there?'

'I don't know,' she said. 'All I know is that it was a wonderful feeling. You were there. There was me. And a lot of flowers!'

She never really talked about the two of us getting married because it often made her think about her parents and the kind of life she lived with them. It had been a year that she had called her parents. They *often* did. For them, she was a commodity to be married off, in a family that would accentuate their name, and more importantly—their business.

According to then, Avantika was a disgrace to their family. A year ago, they had disowned her when she had decided not to get married to the guy they had chosen for her. No, Avantika hadn't told them about me. There were times when Avantika used to be really scared for me. *They could get you killed*, Avantika had said once. These conversations were really not my favourite.

'Hmm,' I said, finding nothing to add to her wedding dream.

'So plans?' she asked.

'Hmm . . . can we still go to Goa?' I asked.

'Nah, I just realized after two months of office that all I want is to spread my legs and relax,' she said.

'Spread your legs?' I smirked.

'Shut up!'

'*You* said it!'

'But I didn't mean it the way you took it, Deb.'s

'Umm . . . *Di* called when you were asleep. We can go to her place,' I said.

Didi was my crazy ass elder sister who got married a couple of years back. She knew about me and Avantika. There were more than a few reasons for me to believe that she loved Avantika more than she loved me.

'I know! She called me in the morning too. But I didn't give it a thought! Yes, we can. That would be nice.'

My sister called her *before* she called me? That was interesting!

'You want to go?' I asked her.

'I would love to go. It's like *ages* since I met her. And she has been asking for so long to meet up.'

'That is probably because Arnab is out on a tour.'

'Shut up, she just likes me so much,' she said flicking her hair and giving me an arrogant look. 'And you are just jealous?'

'Oh . . . please. Keep me out of such TV soap feelings!'

'Whatever! So when do we leave?' she asked.

'Let us leave tomorrow.'

'Right now?'

'As you say,' I said, like a puppy would.

Who would even try arguing with a girl with brown almond eyes and face so radiant that I rarely ever switched on lights when she is around. Though my reasons for not switching on the lights were multi-fold!

There was no way I could love any one as much as I loved her. It was hard to even think about anyone else. She was *the* one. It wasn't that I was waiting for her. She was the one who made me start the wait: the wait to see her again every time she went away, the wait till I got to talk to her again, every time we kept down the phone, the wait till I held her again, the wait to see her smile, the wait to make her kiss me.

The wait . . .

$$\backsim$$

'I am so excited,' she said.

We took the next bus to Pune. Di had been living there since she got married and the wedding was the only time she met Avantika.

'*Why?* I have spent eighteen years with her and let me tell you, she is boring.'

'Did I ask you anything?' she said.

'By the way, Kabir called when you were loading your baggage. He wanted to know our plans for the day. I told him we are going to Pune,' I said.

'Why didn't you give me the phone?'

'You were busy.'

'Oho!' she said and started tapping her phone. I was miffed at her eagerness. Luckily enough, the call didn't connect.

'You seem to be pissed,' she said and smiled.

'You know why!'

'No, let's talk about it.'

'I don't want to. It is better that we don't talk about a guy who is probably better than me in every sense and likes my girlfriend,' I said referring to Kabir.

There was no doubt really that Kabir looked better than I. A lot of people did. I was just an average looking guy with strange hair and a patch of beard on my chin. I had never been to a gym and didn't have a body of a sportsman. I defined average. The dimple was the only saving grace on my face.

But, people usually missed it, no matter how much I tried to get the point across.

'He doesn't like me,' Avantika said.

'But he is better, right?'

'He is not better for me.'

'But he is better, if you were not with me, he is better.'

Why couldn't she just lie that I was better! I never said Malini had better hair, or wore better shoes. Yeah, she didn't. But still . . .

'Deb, if I were not with you it would not matter. But I am with you and for me, you are the best. I would prefer shoes from a street side shop than a Gucci that doesn't fit me.'

'The *difference* is that much, haan? Gucci and a street side shop?'

'You are making me angry now,' she said, her eyes widening to show it.

'Just kidding!'

'Better. By the way, how do you know he likes me?' she asked out of curiosity.

'I just know. It is evident.'

'But he has a girlfriend, Deb. And that is all he talks about.'

'So what? I can tell by the way he looks at you and drools. Who would not?' I said.

'I don't know. Which means *you* drool at other women too?'

'I am yet to come across girls who are half as hot as you are. And I never move around without you. It is good for my ego to have you by my side. But yes, put Angelina Jolie with nothing on, that might stir something more than emotions,' I smirked.

'Good for you. I think there is an empty seat there. I will go there and from now on you can think of *her* and stir whatever you want to,' she said irritatingly.

'What? Why are you being angry?'

'No baby. I am not angry. I just want the best for you,' she smiled and she tip-toed her fingers up my thigh. 'So who are you thinking about *now*? Angelina Jolie?' she smirked.

'Cancel Pune, let's go back.'

'I am kind of nervous,' Avantika said as the taxi rolled over in front of Di's place.

'It is not the first time you are meeting her . . . And as you said, she loves you!'

'You wouldn't understand.'

'Try me,' I said as I unloaded our bags, *hers* mostly.

'It is different now. I met her once, and that too when I was in college. It has been years.'

'Twice, at the wedding too,' I added.

'That doesn't count.'

'It does. She liked your gift the best among hundred others.'

'Deb . . . but she knows we are together now.'

'You and your strange fundas!' I told her.

'And as usual, you are of no help at all,' she said and led the way.

I rung the bell and heard footsteps walking towards the door. It had been nearly a year that I had seen her. I had missed being around her, and I realized that when I heard the door click, my lips curved into a smile.

'Oh . . . look who is here! Finally got time?' she taunted.

'Yeah. And you have grown fat.'

'That doesn't work. I am still lighter than you,' she smiled back. 'Come in, Avantika. I like your scarf!'

She made us sit on the couch.

'See, I don't really have to be formal with you two. So ask for anything, and the fridge is there, so help yourselves,' Di said and went into the kitchen to instruct the maid.

I saw that she and Arnab were doing pretty well for themselves. The house was decked up with things around the world and she looked great! Happy and content.

'So Avantika, how did you like Mumbai?' she asked.

'It was good, better than Delhi for sure. But I love this place too. It is so quiet.'

'I know. He always wanted a house away from the city,' Di smiled.

'How sweet!' Avantika said.

'So, where are you two planning to settle?' Di asked.

That question was strange enough to bring a smile to my face but brought a fade pink blush to Avantika's fair cheeks.

'C'mon, don't kid me. You guys have obviously thought about it,' she said.

'Delhi.'

'Mumbai.'

I and she said respectively. We looked at each other, a little surprised that we hadn't talked about it. Actually we *had*. But in our talks it was either in Singapore or Mauritius. Skyscraper lit skies and the blue seas around us.

'Hmm . . . That was interesting. Deb, Delhi? Avantika, Mumbai?' she smiled.

We looked at each other trying to convince, through mere looks, where we were going to finally settle. Not a surprise that her eyes won. Those big eyes. Ah!

'Mumbai is not that bad,' I said.

Di laughed.

'What?' I asked.

She kept laughing.

'*What?*'

'You know what, Deb? You are not married, she doesn't cook for you, your clothes still don't magically get washed by themselves, and still . . . she pretty much owns you.'

'I . . . am . . . it's not *that*,' I mumbled.

'Okay, whatever. That is your room. I am a little tired with all the cooking. I will go catch a nap. And please don't be loud,' she chuckled and walked away.

We sat there looking at each other and smiled.

'I like your sister, she is fun,' she said as she unpacked stuff.

'What is so much fun about her?'

'I don't know. It is just that had she been a guy, I would have dated her,' she smiled.

'Blah.'

'Aww . . . but I already found a guy form of her, you!' she said and hugged me.

'That is better.'

'You know what is better, though?' she turned me around.

'What?'

'I really like this bed,' she said, looking with that drunken look in her eyes.

'I thought you said the kitchen slab.'

'I like that too,' she said, licking my lips.

'I thought you like the bathtub.'

'I like that as well,' she licked my ear.

'Why don't you say you like *me*?' I smirked.

'I don't. I just *lust* you,' she kissed me and I felt her hand going around me.

Finally.

~

She was knocking on the door for quite some time now, I could say. Avantika woke me up and we scrambled for our clothes.

'So, finally you two are up?' she said waiting at the table for both of us.

I glanced at the clock. We were inside that room for four hours. It was ten.

'Avantika?'

'Yes, *Di*?'

'. . . Don't make it so obvious,' *Didi* said and pulled Avantika's hair from her t-shirt.

Avantika smiled shyly.

'I don't know what you see in my brother! You're so pretty.'

'*Di*, I have always told him that.'

'Are you two ganging up against me? And anyway, I have dated pretty girls before her,' I smirked.

'Guys are such assholes,' *Di* said. 'And I know all the girls you dated before her . . . Naah . . . she is a lot better than them.'

'Thank you, *Di*,' Avantika said and showed the middle finger to me.

'Whatever. There must be something in me that she fell for me!' I tried helplessly to redeem some pride.

'Look Deb, you are ordinary and that is *exactly* why I fell for you,' she said.

Everything was in good humour but it still hurt. You do

not call a blind man blind! Similarly, I was aware there was nothing special about me. I didn't want anyone to tell me about it. Especially not my girlfriend! Avantika saw my eyes droop, even though I was smiling.

'Naah *didi*, Deb is *the* best. In many ways, some of those which I can tell you, some of them which I can't,' she winked.

'Oh . . . little Deb is a man now?' Di smirked.

'And he isn't that *little* anymore. Been there done that, as Deb would say.'

She winked and they both chuckled. Didi said she could do without discussing her little brother's sex life and the topic moved to other areas.

He is not that little anymore! I was smiling. I was no different from any other guy. Tell any man that he has a big penis, and they would be smiling for days. Please note, girls!

Didi said it was late and we should eat. We had been hungry. We had just spent four hours making out and I was dead tired. We all settled down and the servant served us in prodigious quantities. We did not say no. The food was great! *Didi* attributed it to Arnab's fat salary that paid for the fabulous cook.

'The food is awesome *Di*,' Avantika appreciated.

'I know, I tell him that all the time,' Di pointed towards the cook and we chuckled.

We ate a lot and were awesomely full. We were about to get up when didi looked at me and said, 'Hey, I have something for you!'

She got and disappeared into her room. Avantika and I looked at each other, clueless. A little later, she came out with an envelope in her hand.

'Here,' she handed over an envelope to Avantika. 'A small gift from Arnab and me for the two of you!'

'What? We do not need this . . . you don't have to,' Avantika said as she opened the envelope and shouted out of excitement, '*What?* We need *this*, Di! You are so awesome!'

'What is *it?*' I asked.

'Two tickets to Goa!' Avantika shrieked. 'I now know why I fell for you. I wanted a sister-in-law like her.'

She hugged my sister. It was hardly a comforting feeling to see Avantika's breasts pressed against anything but my chest, but seeing her giggling was such a kick. It felt almost as if she was a part of our family. My sister's acceptance was the first step, probably the easiest step but an important one.

'It is my pleasure, Avantika. If you think Deb is not worth enough, I know some very good-looking guys here. Tall, dark . . .'

'Deb is tall, dark and . . .' Avantika said as she looked at me. It was just out of those English movies, when the bride says to her father, *I know dad . . . he is the one.*

I did not know what to do but stupidly smile.

'I wouldn't say anything to that!' Di said. 'Look then, I am sleeping now, you guys can do whatever you want to. Don't wake me up. More importantly, don't wake the neighbours up. Be good.'

She wished us good night and went to her room.

'I simply *love* your sister,' Avantika gushed as soon as she left.

'Yes you made that pretty evident.'

'I want to marry you,' she said.

'Because you love my sister?'

'Yes,' she said. 'I would have gotten my brother to marry her if she was younger and he was older.'

'If wishes were horses, beggars would ride!'

'You are calling me a beggar?' she said as she hugged me.

'Not yet. You are still not in skimpy rags.'

'Deb! Can you *not* be lusty at some time of the day?'

'Hmm . . .'

'Can you spend one day not talking about it?' she asked.

'Can *you?*' I asked her.

'Next topic please,' she said.

'I won! Can we kiss already?'

'Just because you win,' she said and kissed me. 'Who told her about Goa?'

'I did.'

'I love you.'

We kissed and hugged each other tight. Our stomachs were too full for anything else. I would be lying if I said it was inferior to having sex.

'Remember the first time we met?' she asked.

'Yes, when you thought I was dumb and ugly?' I mocked.

'Hmm . . . I never thought we would end up like this,' she said and ran her hands through my hair. I looked at her.

Her eyes had the reflecting pool of all what I had seen in the last few years. I used to look into those every time I was confused about something. They told me everything. Over the last three years, she had always been around, guided me, loved me and hated me. It had been an eventful journey.

Even after three years, she was the first thought of my day. She entered my day with the first morning rays and left with the moonlight. She ruled my life. Her smiles made my day. Her words filled my mornings. Her talks filled my evenings. Her touch made every night unforgettable.

'Neither did I, Avantika. I never believed in fate or destiny before I met you. But you made me believe in those,' I flicked away the hair that came in front of her eyes. 'Why else would you be with me?'

'Why not?'

'I was never the right guy. Moreover, you were the *right* girl for millions of guys out there. Guys who are better than me. Girls like you don't fall in love with guys like me.'

She held my hand and said, 'Words. Deb, words. That is what you have and that is what a girl needs. After a few years, even if you are not as cute as you are right now, your words would still do the magic they do now. They would still make me feel beautiful and wanted. You are all I need, Deb . . .'

No matter how much time passed between us, we still knew what to say to each other to make the other person feel like heaven. We hugged, with tears in our eyes, and our hearts filled with love and with memories of yesterday and fond images of tomorrow.

The next day, we left for Goa.

'I can't believe you just did that,' I said in my slurred speech. We were sloshed.

'I didn't do it alone!' she said. She was drunk too! Her eyes were red and she stumbled over a dog.

'But it was you. You initiated it!' I accused her.

We had just made out in a nightclub's warehouse. There is something in Goa that just makes you so *horny*. Moreover, if you're dating someone like Avantika, it's unlikely that you wouldn't make out everywhere that you go!

'He was looking!'

'Who?' she asked as we lay down on the beach yards away from where the water washed up. It was three in the night.

'The bartender!'

'I don't give a fuck . . . But did you like it?'

'Like hell!' I said. 'But how much did you pay him to open the warehouse for you? The bartender?'

'I kissed him!' she shrieked.

'What?'

'On the cheek!'

'Ah . . . fine,' I said. '*Worth* it.'

'Totally,' she said and we lay on our backs. We looked at the starlit sky and listened to the roar of waves. We were the only ones there. The beach was deserted.

'Deb?' Avantika broke the silence.

'Yes?'

'Do you want to do *it* here?' she looked at me with those drunken eyes, and lingered her fingers on my face. My answer was already in the affirmative.

'I have heard it's dangerous. Goa police is pretty strict about it!'

'Is that a yes or no?'

'When has that *ever* been a no?'

I pulled her by the neck . . . She broke out of my embrace and walked towards the water. My head still spun from the alcohol. By the time I stood up, she was in knee-deep water. She turned and looked at me. Moonlight shone on her. Slowly, she slipped out of her top. Her sarong was wet and floated on the water; she got rid of them. Only her red innerwear separated her from nakedness. Avantika covered her breasts with her hands, looked away from me and walked deeper inside the water. The water on her fair legs glistened under the moonlight. She kept walking away from me, inviting me, as my unsure wasted steps took me towards her. Her hair blew across her face and the moonlight reflected off her flawless, wet skin.

Her washboard abs. The flat stomach. The most tastefully

shaped breasts. The milky white sculpted thighs and calves. I was losing my head. Soon, I stood next to her. She removed her hands from her breasts and put them around my neck. We walked further away from the shore. The lights on the beach were now at a distance where we could hardly see them. We were neck deep into water. There was water all around us. We breathed heavily. Incoming waves splashed water all around, she looked even more seductive as small water droplets clung to her face, and her wet hair stuck on her shoulders. It was just the two of us in an open wide sea, water, moonlight and lust engulfed us. We kissed.

The Goa trip was fabulous beyond words.

The nights under the star lit sky on the deserted beaches, walks on the shores,

Lying next to each other until the sun rose . . . till it set again, the kisses in the neck deep water,

The pastas I loved, the pastas she hated for having had too much of them,

The stolen kisses everywhere, places we lay bare.

The hired bike and unchartered hikes,

My shorts, her sarongs, my favourite tunes, and her loved songs.

The late night walks and the aimless talks,

The holding of hands, the waking up to the morning bands.

The pointless staring, the clubs, the cocktails and the music blaring.

The churches, the shacks, the strangers.

The vodka, the cocktails, the hangovers.

It all seems a blur now. *Unreal.*

Two days, life had stood still. We fell in love again. We celebrated it. We did it like we had never done before.

And Didn't I Just Hate Him?

The train journey back from Goa was uneventful except the huge fight we had over Kabir. I was being unreasonable. Kabir had called up. The company we had done our internship in had offered both Kabir and Avantika jobs in the same department. It was a little hard for me to accept that the two of them will be working together after a year!

Kabir had even asked if they could find a place together in Mumbai to live together later. Avantika said she would talk about it when the time comes. She should have shot it down, there and then! And how could he ask something like that! He knew that Avantika was dating me. We slept that night without talking to each other. Train journeys are extremely romantic, but the fight had just killed it. We came back to Delhi.

We had the most hectic semester staring right at our faces. Things were a little easier for Avantika. She had better grades and she already had a job! I scrambled inside the class at the last second and looked for Avantika. I had overslept.

'This class?' the strategic management professor grumbled.

'Yes sir,' I said meekly. I still looked for Avantika and was confused to where I should sit.

'Firstly, you are late for the class! And then you can't find a seat to sit?' he said. 'No attendance. You can leave if you want to.'

'Okay sir.'

'Sit anywhere and stop disturbing the class,' he said sternly.

I sat on the first bench and cursed myself. I got up, brushed and reached my class at eight . . . and no attendance! *Not the brightest starts to a semester*, I thought. I still tried to spot Avantika from the corner of my eyes but I could not. I texted her and asked where she was.

Right behind you. Last bench.

I waited for the professor to write something on the board so that I could look back.

Last bench . . . she sat right next to that son of a bitch, Kabir! She was laughing. *Nice.*

It was a terrible start to the semester. I had missed attendance and Avantika was sitting with the guy I hated the most. I texted her something random. She replied in a very few words. The other few messages met with the same treatment. I stopped sending them, and my neck kept turning back to look at them. I heard them laughing again. *Bastard.*

'You two,' the professor pointed at the last bench. The class looked at Avantika and Kabir.

'Get up,' he said.

They were still smiling.

'Can you please share the joke with us too?' he bellowed.

Avantika looked down, embarrassed, though I could tell that she was still smiling.

'Get out,' the professor said.

Kabir immediately collected his books, pushed back his chair and left. Avantika followed. They were still laughing when they left the class.

'If anyone has any more jokes to share they can do that outside the class,' he said and got back to telling us about some consulting project of his. I sat there and tried to concentrate on what the professor said to keep my mind off what Kabir was doing with my girlfriend. *Where would these two be? What would they be doing?* I was being paranoid but I could not help it.

I could not shake the thought off my head. Time *stopped*. Five minutes seemed like fifty. I fiddled with my pen and fidgeted with my hair. It got hard to keep sitting in the class. The last few minutes of that lecture were the most painful ones I had ever been through.

I messaged her asking her where she was. *Room*, the reply came. I felt relieved and slowed down my steps as I entered the girls' hostel.

Room No. 203

I opened the door to her room. I hadn't bothered to knock.

Fuck!

Kabir was there! I looked around. I could not find her. My head felt like it would explode.

'Where is she?' I asked him. *What the fuck are you doing here!*

'She has gone to the washroom,' he said as he flipped through Avantika's magazines. That bastard had made himself at home in Avantika's room. *How can he even touch the magazines that she touched!*

'Deb, did he ask for our roll numbers?' he asked.

'I didn't notice,' I said and went out in the corridor. I walked around the corridor and waited for her.

'Where the fuck were you?' I asked as soon as I spotted her.

'In the room,' she said casually.

'Get *him* out of here right now!'

'What? Why?' she asked.

'Because I am asking you to do so.'

'Don't be such a kid, Deb'

'Just do it, Avantika.'

'Okay, I will do that,' she said, a little miffed.

I waited outside the room for him to leave and he walked out after a couple of minutes. I was being unreasonable but I could not bear the sight of that man. I *hated* him with every cell of my body.

'What was he doing *here*?' I asked her.

'Nothing. We were just talking,' she said.

'Here? Is *this* the only place you got? In the whole campus?'

'It is hot outside, Deb.'

'Did he suggest this place?'

'Yes, kind of.'

'Why didn't you say no?'

'Why should I?' she asked innocently.

'As if you don't know what he wants from you!'

'He doesn't. Why are you being so possessive?'

'Possessive? You bring a guy to your room and you expect me not to react?'

'Deb, what do you think he was doing here?'

'I don't know! You tell me!' I accused her.

'Deb, if you think I had some wrong intentions, I don't think we should have this conversation. Do you really think—?'

'I am not saying anything. But we just fought over him just yesterday! Is that not a problem?'

'I trust you, Deb. You don't . . .'

'That is because I don't keep hanging around with random

girls and get them to my room.'

'Kabir is a friend.'

'Raghav has never come to your room and he is a better friend of yours. Nor did Ravi or Kumod! Why *him*?'

'I am not talking about this,' she said and looked away.

'How convenient.'

I left and banged the door behind me. She must be crying now, I thought. And like every egotistical guy, I didn't go back. I acted like an asshole. I did not like it but I hated *him* more.

I ran through the conversation again in my head. Kabir would have laughed at me if he were to know about our fight. She would not message me, I knew. I was wrong and she waited for me to make it right. I did not want to accept defeat so easily. I made my way to Nescafe. Shashank had called, I remembered.

'How was Goa?' he asked.

'It was okay,' I said, my voice did not match up to his enthusiasm.

'Something happened?'

'Not really. Just a little fight.'

Mittal walked beside us with plates of noodles in his hands. Mittal's first name was Ganesh, but he preferred to be called by his last name, he said the name Ganesh reduced his sex appeal.

'Two love lost Romeos. What's happening ladies?' he asked.

Mittal was like the ultimate *anti-love* guy you would ever come across. He was not anti-relationships. In fact, there wasn't a time in the year he wasn't seeing anyone but he always disregarded the need of them. It's just how you get laid, he used to say.

'Heard you went to Goa? Got laid? With your girlfriend?

Now that's new and exciting!' he said mockingly.

'*Di* gifted the tickets,' I said.

'Oh . . . involvement of family . . . very interesting indeed!' he laughed out and suddenly shrieked, 'Look *there!*'

'What?'

'Where?'

'There.'

Mittal pointed out to an exchange student (Catherine!) who had come from Poland. She looked like a porn star! Mittal's and my eyes followed her ass until it disappeared behind a pillar.

Shashank had no such interests. Shashank and Geetika had been going around for five years now. There had been problems in their relationship but they were still going strong. Geetika was a Muslim, and there was no way either of the families would approve of their relationship.

Anyway, being in a relationship never stopped me from feasting at nicely shaped asses and breasts from time to time; Shashank was untouched by this kind of debauchery. He was *loyal*.

'Shashank?' Mittal asked. 'If Catherine . . . is standing naked, right in front of you and offers you a blowjob, would you let her do that to you?'

Mittal knew what the answer would be, and had started smiling.

'Nope,' Shashank said. He knew how Mittal would keep selling the idea to him and smiled.

Mittal continued selling the blowjob, 'Shashank! Catherine! Imagine her naked, her huge red lips, her mouth inviting you; she would suck it good. It will be the *best* blowjob of your life! You would even get to come wherever you want to. Even on her pretty face! How can you turn that down . . . Geetika would not even get to know! You do watch porn, don't you? This is hardly different.'

We both looked at Mittal, shocked. He could be really gross if he wanted to. We really did not want him to describe a blowjob.

'I still wouldn't do it. Not with her at least,' Shashank said and smiled at me.

'Which means you will fuck her mentally, but not physically? That is being such a hypocrite . . . anyway, Deb, what about you?'

'I would do it,' I said. I just did not want to come across as a wimp. I was a hypocrite. Or I was just angry at Avantika.

'Me too!' Mittal said and laughed aloud. 'In fact, I am ready to pay for it too!'

'Oh . . . good that you added the last part and gave some respect to her,' I said.

'She deserves it, Deb. Shashank? Done through the chapter?'

Shashank was our savior in class. He was a year or two younger than we were, and the only sincere one amongst us. He was departmental rank two, and we loved it when he kicked butt of those snobbish kids who slogged throughout the semester. Shashank did not look twenty-three. It seemed he was still in school! He was a kid. His looks were in stark contrast to the person he was. Responsible, straight thinking and very composed.

'Read it yourself. It's not that tough,' he said to us.

'What? Are you crazy? We will not get it. Just read it and tell us what it is all about!' Mittal said.

Shashank narrated the case for the next class. I was only half listening to what he had to say. We rushed to the class minutes before it started. As a reflex, I ran my eyes through the crowd and looked for Avantika until I realized that I was not supposed to do so. We were in the middle of fight!

The three of us found a place for us to sit. Avantika was sitting in the first row and furiously made notes. Kabir sat close by, just a girl between them, and they talked once or twice every few minutes. I suppressed the urge to message her. It was hard to see her even talking to him. I could not even fathom as to why was she . . . I mean she knew that I would be watching her in class. She should have stayed away from him. It just made me sick now.

'Should we get him beaten up?' Mittal whispered in my ear, smilingly.

'Shut up man . . .'

'See, that is why I say. Get only that close to a girl that she warms you not burns you up!' he said seriously. 'You get the pun, right? *Warm* is equal to *sex? Burn* is equal to *jealousy?* Brilliant, right?'

'Shut up . . .'

'If you have a problem with him, why don't you go and talk to her?' Shashank said being concerned.

'I will not. It is the same every time. She will put forth some big words like trust and love and I will lose the conversation again. Why should it be *me* always?'

'Guys are supposed to take the initiative . . . that is how it works,' Shashank said.

'That is how my dick works too. Suck it,' Mittal said. 'This is because we pamper girls! Stop pampering them and their expectations would come down. They will be out of excuses to cry, simple!'

'SILENCE!' the brand management professor bellowed. 'The students who haven't submitted the assignment need to see me after the class.'

The moment he said it, I assumed that I had to go. I looked at these two to see if they had submitted it. They shook their heads and smiled at the sheer audacity! Not only did we miss the deadline, we did not even know what assignment he was referring to. The class ended and the professor named out the students who had not submitted the assignment. My name wasn't there. Mittal and Shashank looked at me as if they had caught me in a threesome with their sisters. I had violated a *Bro*code. I had submitted an assignment when they hadn't.

'Avantika,' I explained.

They let out a sigh.

'If you two are fighting, can I ask her out? I really need someone to do my assignments too,' Mittal smirked.

'Lucky dog . . .' Shashank said. 'That is why I said, there are some places girls take the initiative, where you never would.'

'Oh Shashank, stop bullshitting! We don't need such statements from a guy who even takes the initiative to wash his girl's clothes.'

'I just picked up laundry once,' he said in defense.

'As if you wouldn't have washed them too, had *she* asked! You would have washed her maid's clothes too, if given the chance,' he smirked.

'Anyway Deb, the fight ends?' Shashank asked.

'I don't know,' I said.

What does one do when you girlfriend is like the sweetest little thing on the whole planet? You just feel that you are the stupidest guy in the whole world. I was the stupidest guy with the sweetest girl one could ever have.

She left the class and Kabir left closely behind. Not the prettiest of scenes for me, but I had the first right on her, so I brushed Kabir aside and asked her if we could talk. I followed her to the coffee shop inside our college and we started to talk.

'Thank you,' I said.

'For what?' she asked. The coffee froth perched playfully on her pink lips. She licked it away.

'For the assignment,' I said, apologetically.

'You never thanked me before for it,' she said, trying hard not to show that she was smiling.

'We never fought this bad before . . . I guess.'

'It is okay, baby,' she said, ran her palm over my cheek. Her one touch and I was her puppy again.

'I am sorry.'

'It is fine,' she said. 'Come,' and led me by her hand to her room.

'So?' I asked after we reached her room.

'What?'

'What *what*?' she said.

'I mean *why* your room?'

'. . . because unlike some people I think people do a lot more than just kiss each other all over behind a closed door. They can discuss corporate finance too, you know!' she chuckled.

'I get your point. It is just that I am not comfortable. A little insecure, I mean who wouldn't be if he is dating a stunner like you?'

'Aww . . . that's sweet. But I love you, Deb. Why don't you understand that? Why do you still doubt me?'

'It is not as if I doubt you. It is just that I do not want Kabir to feel that he has a chance with you. I know this is silly, but I can't help it.'

'I know baby,' she said and hugged me.

'Would you not feel bad if I hang around with Malini?'

'Not at all, Deb. I trust you. I really do. I do not trust her, but that is another thing. I know you would always be with me,' she said and pecked me.

'I *always* will.'

'Now go away from my room. I got to study. Go and meet your Malini!' she said and pushed me out. I scratched my head as I stood outside her room.

Why bring me all the way to your room and not make out? What happened to the concept of patch-up sex!

How Far Were We Into This?

Mittal shouted as soon as he saw me in the corridor, 'Had sex and solved everything?'

Everybody turned and looked at him. I grounded my teeth and widened my eyes to make him shut up. He always made us look like some sex-obsessed group in college.

'What happened?' Shashank asked.

'Nothing much . . . We talked and everything is normal.'

'What?' Mittal exclaimed as he lit a cigarette. 'You talked? You were in her room . . . Why didn't you just sleep with her? That is how you tell the girl is still yours.'

'I don't have to do that,' I said. 'No thank you,' I turned down his cigarette.

'Have a cigarette, dude . . . See these are just like girls. Put onto your lips, it feels great. A few minutes later, it just burns out. Then you need another one! And another one. That is how girls are. You fall in love with them and slowly, it becomes a habit. Navy cut one day, Marlboro the other. You cannot kick the habit. But you feel good about it every time you puff one! Or *fuck* one!'

'Where does he get such ideas from?' Shashank said.

'I wish I knew,' I said.

'You know it is so sad that both my friends suck so much. Life is beyond love, guys! It is beyond running after girlfriends . . . Beyond giving them gifts and aligning your life according to them . . . Shashank, when was the last time you went out with a girl who was not Geetika? Three years?'

'Four,' he replied.

'See? How do you know she is the one for you when you don't even consider other girls?'

'See, that is where you are wrong Mittal. I don't feel the need. I just want to be with her,' Shashank said. He always talked beyond his age and his looks.

'See? You are wimps. Both of you! You are scared. You are scared that you are not men enough to get more than what you already have.'

'I still agree with what Shashank said. I don't feel the need,' I said.

'I am not asking you fuckers to start sleeping around with everything that moves on two legs and has breasts,' Mittal defended himself.

'Then what do you want us to do?' I asked.

'Just go out! Have some fun and give yourself a friggin' chance!' Mittal blabbered.

'I think we really need to do the Marketing assignment now,' Shashank said and I nodded.

Mittal flapped opened the laptop irritatingly. He was pissed that we were unmoved. He desperately wanted us to sleep around. *Why?* We never knew. It is a *guy thing*, I guess. If a friend gets laid, it's like you getting laid!

We had hardly started studying when Mittal's' phone

beeped and he left the room. Mittal *never* took those calls in front of us. Shashank and I had tried but never succeeded in finding who the mysterious girl was . . . Or the mysterious girls . . .

'Who do you think it is?' I looked at Shashank. He shook his head and got back to his books.

Mittal had never formally introduced us to any of the girls he went out or slept with! Every few days, a *new* hot girl would leave his hostel room with her hair ruffled, lipstick smudged and with a love bites on her neck, but he never let us talk to anyone. It was creepy.

'I don't want you guys to be friends with any of the girls I go out with,' he had once said.

'Why?' I had asked.

'I don't want to get caught. I lie to them all the time. I don't want them calling you and asking about me! Naah! I can't let that happen,' he had explained.

He had a point there. Your lies should always be unverifiable! Anyway, we often doubted that Mittal was hiding something. We expected that one fine day, he would break down in front of us and would say something like, *'I was dumped by this girl five years ago and since then all I have been trying to do is to get back to her. I attempted suicide twice.'* Nothing of this sort ever happened. Not even close. For the last twelve months, we had seen more a dozen girls leave that fated hostel room.

'I don't think I can study anymore,' I said.

'You're leaving the rest of it?' Shashank asked.

'Yep,' I said and shut down my laptop. He did the same. Shashank was in bad company. Mittal and I knew that without our unholy influence on him, Shashank would have topped every goddamned exam in MDI! But we loved him too much to lose him to books and marks! We could lose him to blowjobs from porn stars from Poland, but definitely not to Free Market Economics. *Eww.*

'Didn't college get over too soon?' Shashank said.

'Seriously, it has been a year and it hardly feels like it. It should have lasted four years. *At least!*'

'Yea, we wish,' he said wistfully. 'I just hope Geetika gets placed in the same city as mine.'

'Hmm . . . yeah.'

'So what have you and Avantika thought?'

'As in?'

'Are you getting married?'

'Eventually . . . in a few years . . . I mean we intend to. Her parents would object but you know the equation there.'

'Your parents?'

'They wouldn't be too happy about it . . . Hmm . . . I don't know. I guess, if I push them, they would not say no. After all there are so many love marriages around, aren't there?'

'Yes.'

'Hmm . . . So you and Geetika?'

'We can't get married,' he sighed. 'Umm . . . you know.'

Though he had done his graduation from Delhi and that is where he had met Geetika, Shashank hailed from a powerful industrial family based in Meerut.

'My family wouldn't let me marry Geetika.'

'The *Muslim* factor?' I asked. I knew it was the reason. Over their relationship over the many years that they had been together, they had broken up a few times. They knew they would not be together forever. But when there is love, you can't keep two people apart for too long, can you?

'Yes.'

'Hmm . . . so, when are you going to break-up with her?

You have to do it soon, man,' I asked not sure whether I should be asking the question.

'I know . . . but then, it's so hard not to be with each other,' he said with a glint of sadness in his eyes.

Mittal and I had asked him more than a few times to end his relationship with Geetika and make it easier for the both of them. He tried but he could never do it. He was so much in love with her. We realized that Mittal overheard our conversation when he rudely interrupted it!

'You guys are such girls! Twenty three and you want to get married?' Mittal said. 'It is a long way off . . . who knows what happens in six years! By the way, assignment? Where is that going?'

'It is done with,' I said.

'Great. I am going to the gym. See you in an hour,' he said, picked up his gym bag and left. Mittal, a gym freak, and never missed a day. Not even between exams, and it showed. One could mistake his biceps for footballs! He used to walk shirtless in the corridors and enjoy the admiring smiles of both the sexes. Mittal had the most perfect abs I had ever seen. His pictures on Facebook were a rage! No wonder, he had girls drooling all over him. Sometimes, I used to accompany him, but I just could not get rid of the flab!

'Deb, catch you later,' Shashank said as he stuffed his laptop inside his bag.

'Geetika?'

'Yes. It is her birthday tomorrow. So have to buy something for her.'

'You have decided what to get for her?'

'I was thinking of getting her a ring . . . but I don't want to give her a wrong idea,' he said and left.

Wrong meaning? A ring? I had just given a ring to Avantika a few days back. Did it mean that I wanted to marry her . . . *eventually?* For the first time, I realized how deep I was into my relationship. I smiled thinking about it. The whole idea of Avantika and me, together for life, was comforting. However, before it would happen, it would be a long and tiring fight to convince our parents and relatives. *Was I ready?* I thought so. I wanted her to be there.

Shashank and Geetika—I had hardly imagined them without each other. To think that they would not be together was strange. It was a creepy thought to think they would be with different people. *Deb and Avantika?* With different people? That felt downright *sick*. Love makes you so dependent. To imagine my life without Avantika was a ridiculous thought.

If You Do It, So Will I—The Case!

Avantika and I had our differences, but that's what made us special. Avantika had always been an ambitious girl, and she always got what she wanted. She had an unforgettable and painful past. Her previous relationships had been total disasters that saw her spiraling down into a deep dark pit of alcohol and drugs for a couple of years. She had been to a series of rehabilitation centres but she had run from there. She had almost destroyed herself when she found a spiritual connection with Spirit Of Living and Sri Guru. She has not touched drugs since.

My life was a lot different. I had always been laidback and my relationships had been a joke. I had never felt love before I met Avantika and she taught me all about me. My relationships were always bag full of lies! Things changed though after Avantika came around . . . I loved her, I lusted her! I felt every emotion a guy can, for a girl.

Avantika was now a lot different from how I first saw her. Avantika did not have the brightest of childhood and the sunniest of teens. Though her brother doted on her and hated me, her parents always behaved as if they had just one kid. She often said that my love for her saved her. But *who* wouldn't love someone like her!

She had her relapses and slipped into short-term depression states. A few hugs, a few tears and my promises of *forever* used to make it all right. It pained me to see her in pain, and it made me sick when I could not make it better.

I made her wash away every bad memory she had, she said.

Our relationship was like a fairy tale, only *better!* There was unimaginable love, expensive gifts, surprises, road trips and awesome blowjobs. It was scary to think how good we made each other feel. It looked like someone had scripted the most beautiful love story ever. The princess kisses the frog. The frog remains a frog. The princess still decides to dump all princes and stay with frog. She even sleeps with the frog. It cannot get any better than this! It seemed like the frog had himself written the love story. It was just so biased.

'Where is Kabir?' I mocked her as I sat next to her.

'Shut up. He is working on the case study.'

'Case study?'

'*The* Mahindra one? The one you refused saying that it was bullshit?'

'You are still working on it? Who else is in the team?'

'Just the two of us.'

'Oh . . . just you *two?* I winked.

'Yeah . . . Now start the taunts!'

'So when do you have to send it?'

'Today.'

'Oh . . . and what if you get selected?'

'We would go to Mumbai and present the case. IIT-Mumbai, their fest coming up . . .'

'Mumbai? You two?' *What the fuck?*

'Yes. Oh don't start it again,' she said and rolled her eyes.

'No, I won't, but just a little uncomfortable. Never mind, I will too send the case study, with Malini,' I smirked.

'Oh . . . you won't work with me, but you will work with *her*, huh?' She smiled.

'Why not? If you can work with Kabir, I can work with Malini!'

'No, I will be happy if you do. At least you will do something!' she said, patted my back and concentrated on the class.

Mumbai? With Kabir? Alone? This cannot be!

I made up my mind to start working on the case study though I knew I would not stand a chance. I was dumb and I could not do it alone.

'So?' I asked Avantika, 'what all have to be put in the presentation?'

Avantika started to tell me what all Kabir and she had done. I had already given up before even starting. I could not possibly match what they had done or even come close.

'You did all that?' I asked, shocked at how much detail they had put into the presentation.

'Yes,' she said and smiled at me.

'. . . and when is the deadline?'

'Tonight!' she said.

Fuck it. I did not matter anymore . . . there was no way I could have made that presentation. We left the class. Avantika looked in a hurry and I asked her where she was running to.

'I have to go meet Kabir and add a few things,' she said.

'Add? *More?*'

'Whatever. Aren't you doing it? With Malini?' she smiled at me.

'Fuck you.'

'Later. I am *busy* tonight,' she said and winked. I saw her leave and meet Kabir in the mess. That *asshole*. Now, she was intentionally making me burn with envy. I could not have accepted defeat! Maybe, I needed to make this crazy presentation. But who? *Malini?*

I toyed with the idea of teaming up Malini for quite some time. If I had to make Avantika jealous, I had to get a *hot* teammate! Malini was perfect for it. She was hot, she was single and she could have made a kick-ass presentation. Of what I knew of her, she was a sharp and intelligent girl with a huge attitude problem. I had never talked to her a lot, but I always felt she was sweet. There was no harm in trying. So that afternoon, I followed Malini as she made her way to her hostel room.

'Malini . . .' I called her name aloud.

'Yes?' she said in her accented voice.

Malini had done her undergraduate college and few years of her school from Canada. She had come back with a heavy accent, an attitude and an incredibly strange and sexy dressing sense. I loved her legs. They shone so much that it seemed like she waxed them every day! She used to go jogging every evening in a pair of shorts and guys used to check her out all the time. Some people thought Malini was slutty but she had never been involved with anyone in college. Malini was a little crazy too. She had red streaks in her hair! No one does that in a management college. With her corpse white complexion, and an amazing body, she hardly looked Indian. Initially, many people had mistaken her for an exchange student. Long story short, she was *hot!*

'There is this case study competition in Mumbai. It is pretty interesting . . .'

'I have read it,' she interrupted.

'Oh . . . nice . . . I have started working on it . . . and it is almost finished . . . I just need a team member—'

'Almost finished it?' she started to walk away from me.

'Yes, almost.'

'Then why do you need *me?*'

'It is a team of two. And you know . . . having a girl in the team helps,' I said and smiled. People had told me in the past that I did not look ugly when I smiled and that my dimple made up for my other sad features. I hoped *it* would work.

'Having a girl helps? That's chauvinistic!' she said.

'Umm . . . err . . .'

'Anyway, you have finished it?'

'Umm . . . to be honest, I haven't started . . .' I smiled sheepishly.

'That is what I thought . . .' she laughed. 'So you want to work on it together?'

'Precisely.'

'See you at 9, mess?' she smiled.

I nodded and she left.

Moments later, I entered my room and found Mittal on my bed. He was smiling. I was sure he had seen me talk to Malini.

'Giving yourself a *chance?*' he said.

'What?'

'Remember I told you? Other girls? Fuck, do you even listen to what I say?'

'What other girls? Malini? No!'

'No? What was that then? You and her? Middle of the mess?

You guys were smiling!'

'We are just working on a case study together,' I said. *Case study? Me?* It sounded a little weird!

'Case study? YOU?'

'Yes.'

'Don't make me laugh man,' he said and looked at me. I was serious. 'What bullshit, Deb?'

'Yes . . .'

'What is the deal man?' he asked me in disbelief.

'Nothing . . . Avantika is participating with Kabir. So, I thought I would participate too.'

He looked at me with widened eyes and said, 'Deb? You know that you are psychologically imbalanced, right? You are doing a case study because she is doing the same with him?'

'Not really.'

'Fuck you . . . as if I don't know. Why are you being so possessive? If she wants to be with him . . . let her! You cannot keep sticking to her all the time. This is so . . . disgusting,' he exclaimed.

'It is not that, I just want to be around her,' I defended.

'It's exactly that. You just don't trust your girlfriend.'

'I do.'

'Why Malini then? Why not some guy? Shashank?'

'It is something between Avantika and me.'

'Whatever. Anyway, what did Malini say?' he asked.

'She said yes!' I said.

'She did? I thought she had loads of attitude—'

'Nah, she is sweet,'

The phone rang. It was Malini. She wanted to meet me. It was three hours too early. As I left the room, Mittal's words kept ringing in my head. Maybe, I did not trust Avantika. Or maybe I did. It had been three years now, I knew she would *never* do anything that would hurt me. All said and done, I still did not like Kabir hanging around my girlfriend. She was *mine,* and I wanted to keep it that way.

I reached her room. It was spotless clean like Avantika's room was but still it looked different. The lights were dim and yellow; there were cushions and beanbags that crowded her room. It really looked like a mini bar! I liked her room. It was different from the other rooms of the hostel that used to be crowded with big management books and magazines. *Boring.*

'I read the case,' Malini said.

'Aren't we like three hours too early?'

'I didn't feel sleepy enough, so I read it,' she said.

I looked at her and it seemed like she had tried to sleep. Malini was in a short nightdress that ended mid-way through her thighs. *There is no harm in looking,* I said to myself.

'So, shall we start?' she asked.

'Sure,' I said.

'Should we study here? Or the library?' she asked.

'Here,' I said. I swear to God my intentions were innocent. I know I was staring at her ever since I entered her room, but I had no shady intentions! Now, I felt sorry for my outburst with Avantika when I had found Kabir in her room. They were innocent, so was *I.* Malini handed over the papers that I had to study and I started reading it. We had just started to study when she broke the silence.

'Want something?' she asked.

'Umm . . . err . . .'

'Vodka, gin . . . hmm . . . whiskey?' she asked.

I did not know what to say. She got up from where she sat and pulled out a mini freezer from below her bed. I was speechless as I saw her choose between tiny bottles of whiskey, vodka and other liqueurs.

'Anything?' she asked and dangled a mini bottle of vodka.

'Umm . . . no,' I said.

'Fine,' she said and made herself a drink.

For the first time in my life, I had seen a cool box in a hosteller's room, neatly tucked in behind the bed. That is just what was missing in her room! *Alcohol!*

'Let's start. I will just write the brief overview of the case, you start with the impact,' she said as she sipped on her drink. It was a lot of vodka . . . with *nothing*! We started to work on our slides. It was as if she was drinking and I was getting drunk. Her concentration did not waiver, but mine did. I kept looking at Malini, her drink and her glistening legs. I felt *guilty*. An hour passed when she let out a huge sigh.

'Done?' she asked.

'Not really,' I said.

'I need another one,' she poured an equally big drink as the last one. 'How many hours are we left with?' she asked flapping down her laptop.

'Seven to go.'

'Hmm . . . We can take a break then,' she kept the laptop aside and took a large sip of the drink. 'So, Deb, isn't Avantika participating in this one?'

'She is.'

'But not with you?'

'With Kabir.'

She smiled wickedly. It seemed as if she knew why I was

participating in this event.

'So love her a lot, huh?'

'You can say so,' I said. It always kills me to tell pretty girls that I was taken. It sucked. But then, it was a small price to pay to be with someone as great as Avantika.

'Sweet!' she said. I could sense the sarcasm in her voice.

'Hmm . . .'

'How long has it been for the two of you?' she asked and her phone rang. 'Wait a minute.'

She left the room. I logged into Facebook and waited for her to come back. Ten minutes. Twenty minutes.

'Hey,' I called up Avantika.

'What's up? Are you out somewhere? Went to your room too . . .'

'I am in Malini's room. The case study thing . . .' I said.

'Oh you took it seriously? *Nice.* In her room? Nice moves, boyfriend!' she mocked and chuckled.

'Hmm . . . Where are you?'

'I am in the library, with Kabir. *LIBRARY. NOT MY ROOM.* Now, who is the culprit?' she mocked.

'I am sorry for that. Now can you please shut up?'

'If you insist. So how is the presentation shaping up?' she asked.

'Hey . . . I am sorry,' Malini said as she entered the room. 'Let's get started . . . sorry for the call . . .'

'It is going fine. Will catch you later . . .' I said and we cut the phone.

'Talking to Avantika?' she asked.

She had started to sound a little drunk. I looked at the glass she was drinking from. It was empty. By then, she was about half a bottle down. *Neat.* She picked up the laptop and started to tap furiously on it. She did not talk too much. For the next four hours, she concentrated on the work, much more than I did, often prodding me to work harder. She looked a little upset but I could not ask her why. We were not even friends so I let her be.

'Done?' she asked as she scrolled through the entire thirty-eight slides.

'I think so.'

'Wait,' she tweaked the background of the slides and asked, 'Now?'

'Better.'

'Wait then,' she changed something again. 'Now?'

'It's all the same to me.'

'Now we are done,' she attached the file in the mail and hit the send button. We looked at each other and smiled. It was certainly a feat for me; six hours and I had not moved an inch from where I was sitting. Avantika would be so proud to hear that.

'Calls for a drink?' she asked.

'Sure.'

No bad intentions still, I was genuinely happy. I wanted to call Avantika up and ask how much they had done.

'Vodka?'

'Yep,' I said.

She had been gulping it neat so I thought it would be *girlish* of me to ask for something to accompany mine.

'You drink a lot, do you?' I asked.

'I used to drink in Toronto. I have reduced now,' she said and smiled at me.

'By the way, thank you for the help.'

'Thank you? It is our case study,' she gulped down her drink.

She behaved as if it was like water.

'True,' I said and gulped mine. The vodka burnt my throat, my stomach and my face distorted. It was horrible.

'Too strong?' she asked and smiled.

'Understatement,' I said, the taste still singed my tongue.

'You are a kid,' she said.

'*Really?* Don't throw me a challenge!' I said.

Well, she did . . . and I lost. I was drunk and tippy way before she was. However, we had forgotten about the challenge and had started to blabber about our lives to each other.

She said she missed Canada a lot. Malini said she did not like her time in India and she could not wait to get back there. I was drunk so I forgot a few things that she said. She had talked about her boyfriend in Canada but I do not remember a thing about him! Oh! Yes, he was Samarth.

'We can do without talking about him,' I said. It was the third time I had asked about him and I could see tears in her eyes.

'Thank you. I think we should sleep now. This is getting to my head,' she pointed to the glass.

'Yes. We have worked too hard for a day. I think I am a little drunk too.'

'A little drunk?' she mocked me.

'Okay—*a lot!* I think I should go,' I said and got up.

'Stay,' she said. I saw pearls of tears at the edges of her eyes. I knew she was about to cry. She added immediately, 'No . . . you should go.'

'Hmm . . . I can stay . . . if you . . .'

I felt sorry for her. No matter how drunk I was, I realized that Malini was lonely out here in college. And her relationship problems weren't helping her either.

'You have done enough Deb. Thank you. Bye,' she said and closed the door on my face.

I left the room and she closed the door behind me. I could still hear her crying and sniffing behind the door. Malini had always been a strange girl. She never talked to many people around and we usually thought of her to be high nosed and snobbish. After all, she drove the biggest car on campus, a sparkling Audi Q7 and that in itself is intimidating. Everybody thought twice before talking to her.

My phone beeped. It was Malini.

Felt good today. Thank you. I hope we did well.☺ *Good night.*

'Sleeping?' I called up Avantika as soon as I left Malini's room.

'Umm . . . no . . .' she said groggily. 'You are done?'

'Yes, just sent it.'

'Good. Sleeping now?' she asked.

'Not really. Not sleepy enough.'

'I wish you could come over,' she said.

'Hmm.'

Guys weren't allowed in the girls' hostel beyond eleven in the night. Girls on the other hand were allowed in the boys' hostel at any time, but they preferred not to be among hairy, shirtless, stinking guys in boxers.

'I wish you were next to me,' she said. The way she said it would have questioned the sanctity of priests' thoughts. I was merely a lusty boyfriend.

'Why do you think I want anything different?'

'Come over then,' she said.

'But . . .'

'Nobody will know . . .'

'But—'

'Yes, you are right . . .' she said dejectedly.

There were no guards but no one really broke the rule. Girls were known to complain about the presence of any guy in their corridors! I guess they all feared cute boys would catch without make-up and in crappy clothes! So the presence of any guy in girls' hostel beyond prescribed time was promptly reported to the college office.

'I will come.'

'But what if—'

'No one will know Avantika. I will dash in and leave in the morning. What say?'

'It is a little risky.'

'When did we stop taking risks?' I asked her. 'And it's not the first time we are doing this.'

'Just don't get caught!' she said and cut the line.

I realized it was a big risk for a night of immense pleasure, but I have often succumbed to temptation and that day was no different. I crossed the well-lit corridor that led to the girls' hostel with unsure steps. If I were to get caught, it would be a huge waste. I just wished I would get to sleep with her before anyone complains. I called Avantika when I was about ten paces from her room. I could already smell her in the air. It was overwhelming, or maybe it was the erection in my pants, that made the world seem a little sexier!

'Clear?' I whispered.

'Wait.' I waited at the foot of the stairs waiting for her to give a go. 'Now!' she said.

I made a mad dash up the stairs and then a left and then a right. I ran right into her room and she closed the door behind her. I panted as I got to her room.

'Not that tough, eh?' she asked.

'Not really,' I smiled.

She held my dangling hand and tugged at it, while I came close. 'So, why are you *here*? Girls' hostel? So late in the night, it's not allowed, is it?'

She was inches away from me and I could feel her breath through my shirt. Anything that was forbidden, like boss' chambers, conferences rooms, deserted beaches, parked cars on a deserted road . . . all this got Avantika's hormones running. So did mine.

'I missed you,' I said as she let her lips hover around mine.

'Did you *drink?*' she asked.

'Kind of.'

'With?' she asked. Now, I was scared.

'Malini. Just one drink. She insisted.'

'But you were in her room all day? Weren't you?' she asked.

'She has tiny vodka bottles stashed under her bed!'

'I think she *likes* you . . .' she asked.

'Ah! She is nice too.'

'Nice? *Nice?*' she pressed onto a love bite from a few days before which still pained.

'*Arre* . . . kidding . . . Don't do that.'

She removed her hand from the love bite. Instead, she came close, planted her lips on my neck, and started to suck on it. She bit, and bit hard enough to leave a mark. A bigger one.

'Now that would leave a hickey,' I said as soon as she left me.

'I want it to,' she said, 'I want a stamp on you that says you are mine.'

I really did not mind love bites from her. It was good for my ego. If people spot it, they thought that I was sleeping with Avantika. *What is better than that?* You are sleeping with the most desirable girl in campus and it is not a rumour! You have a love bite to prove it.

'I should be giving you one too. You know, to tell Kabir that you are mine?'

'I tell him that often. And you shouldn't worry about him,' she said and her voice cracked a little.

'And you shouldn't worry about her,' I said.

'Aww . . . what happened, baby?'

'Nothing,' she said.

'Just say it.'

'It's nothing. I just want you to know that I really need you. I want you to be around. Always.'

'I will be. But why do you say that today?' I asked.

'Deb, you are here now. But tomorrow you might find someone. Someone better than me . . . and when that happens, I don't want to cling on to you.'

'You are talking nonsense, Avantika,' I protested.

'Just keep me around. I will be happy to see you happy,' she abruptly stopped speaking. There were a few days now and then, when she used to feel romantic and said things like these. I loved it when she talked like this. It made me feel wanted and loved. It is a strange emotion for ugly men like me to feel.

'Avantika. I would never find anyone who is as beautiful, as sweet, or as funny as you are. I love you and that is *never* going to change. You taught me what love is, leaving you would mean unlearning all that, and I do not want to do that. I cannot do that. You are part of me now and I cannot let you go. Not even if I want to. You are the only thing I want. You are the only thing I need.'

I would never accept it, but I had tears in my eyes. I felt lucky that I was around her and that she loved me. I had also imagined how life would be without her. *Barren. Loveless. Purposeless.* Deep down, I knew why she said all those things that day. She was not happy that I was working with Malini.

I Swear I Do Not Remember Anything!

'Deb! Saw the mail?' Avantika shouted as I walked up to you.

'What mail?' I asked groggily.

It had been more than a week that we had sent those case studies and I had completely forgotten about it. I had not fancied my chances. I knew Malini was smart but I did not think we stood a chance. My idea was to make Avantika jealous and I had succeeded in doing that. I did not care after that.

'Yours is chosen!' she shrieked.

'Huh?'

'Such a lame reaction!'

'Oh . . . the Mumbai thing? *The case study?* And you?' I asked.

'No,' she said with no tinge of disappointment. 'But you go and win it . . . for me.'

'*What?* I am not going,' I said.

'Why not? You worked hard for it! You should go.'

'Worked hard?' I said. 'I just worked on it for a few hours.'

'Don't bullshit me, Deb. For the first time, you did

something constructive, don't let it go!' she said.

'What do you mean?' I got slightly pissed off at her statement, though there was nothing wrong in what she said. I had never been ambitious and wanted something badly in life. Avantika used to be pissed off at my laidback attitude.

'You know what I meant Deb; you got to take charge sometime. You have to be a little serious about things. You are intelligent and smarter than many people around. You can make a difference. Do something that will make me proud!'

'Do I let you down?'

'I knew you will go there. I am not saying that. Just do justice to yourself, and to me. You are better than this,' she smiled.

'Why do you always have to make so much sense?'

'I was just born smart,' she said, smiled and held my hand. We entered the class.

Kabir was furious that they could not get through. *How did he get through!* Kabir had asked Avantika. She told me that she was not happy that her boyfriend was being ridiculed. Kabir was an asshole.

'So are you going?' Shashank asked.

'Obviously, he is . . . you never know what might happen there, Deb!' Mittal said.

'I don't want anything to happen,' I said.

'Idea!' Mittal said, 'Why don't you go to Goa again? With Malini?'

'Hmm . . .' I said.

'Imagine man . . . a few shots of Vodka and Malini in a

bikini on a beach. Is there anything else you could possibly want?' he said, already drooling.

'That is not what I am thinking right now. It is just that I don't want to go.'

'Aw . . . you will miss Avantika?' Mittal mocked.

'Shut up man,' Shashank said.

'I feel she gets a little insecure when I am around others.'

'*So what?* That shouldn't stop you,' Mittal said disgustingly. 'She should understand, isn't that what relationships are all about?'

'Will you ever stop being an asshole?' Shashank said irritatingly.

'Me? Asshole? That is what you guys are! Get a life,' he smirked and left the room. It was a call again.

'Deb, but I think you should go,' Shashank said. 'I talked to Avantika and she was excited about it! Don't disappoint her.'

'I know . . .'

'Anyway, you didn't mail me the case study?'

'I will do it right now,' I said and opened my laptop.

'But why didn't you ask me to work on it?' he seemed pissed.

'. . . because you don't have boobs.'

'What?'

'I wanted someone who could make her jealous!' I said.

Shashank laughed. He started to look through the presentation and was impressed. I felt good about myself. I now saw what Avantika was trying to tell me. It feels good to have a boyfriend who is not worthless.

Shashank was unreal though. He was so sweet sometimes that it almost made Mittal and me doubt it. It seemed like he had some ulterior motive behind doing the selfless acts he did.

He completed our assignments, filled our forms and called us to make sure we did not miss anything. His motherly behaviour shocked us when we had first got into college but slowly we got used to it.

I called Malini for the hundredth time that day. Finally, she picked up.

'Where are you?' I asked, almost angrily.

'Why do you care man?' She sounded drunk and her Canadian accent was even heavier. 'What's up man?'

Her lingo always somewhat caught me off guard. The extensive usage of *fuck it* and *man* took some time for me to get used to.

'Nothing much, Malini. Just wanted to tell you that our case study is selected . . . Umm . . . and we can go to Mumbai to fight for the top spots.'

'. . . and what about your girl's?'

'Avantika? They didn't get through,' I said.

'Ahh . . . are we really that good?' she said in her slurred speech.

'Maybe! You did most of it . . . so you definitely are good. So we are going?' I asked her.

'No.'

'*Why?*' I asked, puzzled. 'We worked hard for it!'

'See Deb, you wanted to go because she was going with that fuck-all prick . . . So, it doesn't make sense to go now,' she said. I was glad Malini found Kabir detestable. It was only later that I found out that Kabir had hit on her too during the initial days of college.

'But we worked hard for it,' I said. I argued with Malini because I wanted to go now, because Avantika wanted me to go.

'I don't care about it. Neither do you. So just fuck it,' she laughed aloud.

She was drunk that day . . . really drunk. I had to play the cute-boyfriend card again to convince her. I told her that Avantika really wanted me to go and that I wanted to impress her. Finally, after half an hour, she agreed. *We* were going to Mumbai!

~

'Packed everything?' Avantika asked. 'Toothpaste? Foam?'

'Yes baby. How many times will you ask?'

'It's just that . . .' she choked, 'we have never been away for so long, so it feels a little strange.'

'Aww!' I hugged her. 'Don't cry.'

'Do you have a problem?' she said.

'Nope! You look cute when you cry!'

'Just go and win. Don't let me down,' she said. The taxi honked and reached the college gate.

'Hi Avantika,' Malini said.

'Hi Malini.'

'I wouldn't be crying if I were you,' Malini said.

'Why so?' my girl asked.

'He is doing all this for you. You are one lucky girl, Avantika,' she said and smiled at Avantika.

'Isn't he sweet?' Avantika winked at Malini.

We sat in the car and we left for the airport. Avantika did not want to come to the airport for she did not want to see me go.

'I like your girl,' Malini said as she checked her make-up.

'And she likes you I guess,' I smiled, 'There is something so similar between the two of you.'

'Oh . . . so will you fall for *me* now?' she joked.

'Will you?'

'I have a boyfriend . . . if I didn't . . . maybe.'

'Hmm.'

'Avantika is too good for you,' she said.

'I know,' I said, I was used to such statements before.

'So, how did you two land up together?'

'It is a long story,' I said. We got in the line, took our boarding passes, and got ourselves checked. My mind raced back to how Avantika and I had started. We boarded the flight and Malini started that conversation again.

'We have a two hour flight. I think now you can tell me your *long story*!' she said.

'I get air sick,' I said.

'Kid.'

'That's an interesting story!' she said as we entered the Mumbai airport. I had finished my story and she was fascinated.

'I told you!' I said.

'So are they going to send us a car or what?' she asked as we picked our bags from the conveyer belt.

'Malini, we are participants and not the chief guests!' I mocked.

'So do you know how to get there?'

'There must be taxis outside.'

There were *plenty*. We took a taxi and it took us an hour and half to reach the college in the humid weather. We hated it.

We sweated like pigs and the humidity killed all our excitement.

'I am already regretting coming here, Deb. You are an asshole,' she said.

I called up the festival coordinator and he came running to the main gate to receive us. The urgency he showed while directing us to the hostel room that we had to share, impressed us.

'I hope you don't snore,' she said.

'I don't,' I said. 'I hope you don't fart.'

'I do sometimes and people die when I do,' she made a face. 'When is the competition tomorrow?'

'It is at ten, I guess.'

'You want to go through the presentation again?'

'Sure. Shashank has made some changes and I guess they are good.'

'Nice,' she said and flipped open the laptop.

It was already ten in the night, when we finished with the presentation. We divided our parts and we thought we were ready. I was unpacking when Malini's phone rang and she went outside the room to get it. A little later, she had a huge smile on her face.

'Guess what!' she said.

'What?'

'A friend called and she invited me to a party! She saw my status message on Facebook and knew that I was in Mumbai!'

'So?' I asked.

'So? Let's go!' she said, excitely as she rummaged through her luggage.

'I don't know her! And we have the presentation tomorrow,' I said.

'Don't be such a spoilsport! Let's go!' she said. She was already putting dresses on herself to see what looked better.

Fifteen minutes later, we were on the Mumbai streets making our way to Trilogy, a hip lounge bar in Bandra. I had seen its pictures in page three parties' pictures in newspapers; it looked like an expensive place. But Malini was rich and I assumed she had rich friends. During our drive to the club, Malini's phone rang many times.

'So? Who all are coming?' I asked.

'A whole bunch of people!' she said and smiled at me.

Awkward. It was as if her whole friend circle was in Mumbai.

Anyway, we reached the club. The bouncers checked our names in the guest list and let us through. On the table facing the door, about fifteen people waved at Malini! *Girls. Guys. Gays.* Malini ran to them and hugged a lot of them as I walked slowly up to them and hoped the hugging business would end soon. The girls had come in the shortest of dresses possible. Off shoulders. Strap on dresses. Uber-short skirts. I could hardly see their faces in all the darkness but I could see the legs and the shirts shining. All of them seemed to have shopped directly out of fashion catalogues! It was a total eye feast. It felt awkward between all the unknown people but I did not mind the sight.

'This is Deb,' Malini announced

Everybody shouted a big *Hi*, and I greeted them back.

Luckily, everybody was already a little drunk. There were already a few tequila shots lined on the table. They immediately started forcing them down my throat. I did not resist; I wanted the social awkwardness to end as soon as possible. It seemed like getting drunk was the shortest and the easiest way out!

One shot. It hit the head. It burned my throat. The music went louder. The lights hit my eyes. *Second shot.* It hit harder. My stomach burned. The music blurred. *Third shot. Fourth shot. Fifth Shot.* I lost count. It hit everywhere. The stomach calmed. My throat was soothed. The music ran through my body now. The lights seemed to converge into one big blob of different colours. Suddenly, *everybody was a friend.*

I picked up a bottle of beer and gave it a huge glug. It tasted like water and I drank as if it was water. After a while, I was totally disoriented. I do not remember the last time I drank so irresponsibly. It really did not matter what I was drinking. Shots. Beer. Whiskey. I drank *whatever* I could get my hands on.

I felt someone tugging at my arm, and felt the blue and red rays of light pierce my eyes, enter the brain, and play lacrosse with it. My legs moved and so did my hands. I felt arms around me. I felt mine around someone else. Time slowed down. The faces blurred. Everyone looked the same. They all looked seductively beautiful and everyone danced well. The lights dimmed further and I felt bodies writhing against me. *Was it Malini?* Was it her friend in green dress? I do not know. I still cannot tell. Somewhere in all the sweat and writhing of bodies against me, the night ended for me.

'Wake up. *WAKE UP.*'

I heard these sounds ring in my head. Then I felt my shoulder shaking, then the whole of me and the bed with it.

'Huh?' I opened my eyes to see Malini staring at me. Her voice hurt my ears. 'What happened?'

'It's fucking ten!' she said.

'Huh? Ten?' I said, still not registering in my head.

Then it did. *CASE STUDY!*

'Oh . . . fuck, fuck, fuck.'

I stood up, my head hammered by a million sledgehammers.

The taste in my mouth sucked and my lips were parched. It was a terrible hangover. The room was in a mess and so was I.

'When did you wake up?' I asked her.

'Just now.'

'Let's just get ready and rush,' I said. I opened my suitcase and looked for my suit. We looked at each other and realized we did not have enough time to go out and change. We turned our backs to each and dressed up. As we changed in that room, I got a glimpse of her in the mirror on the wall, but it was unintentional. I did not mean to stare at her bare back.

We rushed through the hostel corridors! My head still pounded, my hair was in a mess and I could hardly walk straight. We entered the auditorium and contacted the co-coordinator. He was pissed off for he was trying to reach us since morning.

'Where the hell have you guys been? Now, we have scheduled you last in line,' he said.

We just looked at each other and smiled. While the other teams gave their presentations, we brushed ourselves up and tried to look as presentable as we could. Quite obviously, she did a better job. She had the entire cosmetic industry in her handbag.

'I hope you have the pen drive,' she asked.

'Yes, I do,' I said and we wished the best of luck to ourselves.

We were up next. I would not say we did our best, but we did the best we could with a hangover and thoughts of the day before running through our heads. The result was out. We did not feature in the list of winners. Not even a consolation prize. We lost. I lost.

'Hey . . . what happened? How did it go?' Avantika asked.

'We lost.'

'Oh . . . never mind.'

'But it went well?' she asked.

'Under the circumstances, yes,' I said.

'Under *what* circumstances?'

'We got a little drunk last night, bad hangover this morning.'

Just as I said this sentence, Malini punched me and gave me a nasty stare. *What was that for?*

'You went drinking with her? Again?'

'It was a party.'

'A night before the presentation? How irresponsible can you get?' she scolded. She wasn't happy to hear this.

'I am sorry. I didn't think I would drink that much.'

'Anyway, had fun?'

'I guess . . . I do not remember most of it. I was out within the first three shots.'

'At least you did something well!' she chuckled.

'I guess.'

'Come back soon now,' she said. *Aww!*

'Yes, I will.'

'So what plans for tonight?' she asked. I saw Malini get restless by the long phone call.

'We might go out again.'

'Have fun! But don't do anything silly . . .'

'*Silly?*'

'Nothing, just come back soon, Deb,' she said and cut the phone. I looked at Malini and she looked bored.

'You call her baby?' Malini mocked.

'So? Everyone uses it. What do you call your boyfriend?'

'I call him by his name,' she said.

I chose not to ask anything else about him. She was in tears the last time I had asked about him. I did not have the heart to see her like that again. I let the topic rest and we headed to the nearest bar to celebrate our effort. *Caravan* was a decently done up place for its price and I liked it from the moment I stepped in. We ordered our food and drinks.

'Why did you hit me when I was on the phone?'

'I wanted you to *shut up*,' she said.

'Why?'

'You don't have to tell her everything!'

'What did I tell her?'

'That you got sloshed last night . . . with me.'

'But I tell her everything . . . and she doesn't mind . . . and she doesn't have a problem,' I said.

I had never found a reason to hide anything from Avantika. The guilt and the discomfort used to be too much to bear. I rather preferred not doing things that I would have to hide from her! Avantika was *the* witness to my life. She was someone who would see it all, someone who would know everything about me, someone who will always be there.

'Obviously she minds, *everyone* does. She just does a better job of hiding it.'

'She knows that I wouldn't do anything unwarranted,' I said, confidently.

'Then you're lucky she doesn't know what happened last night!' she smirked.

'Why is that smirk on your face?'

'Nothing,' she smiled.

'What happened last night?' I asked again.

'You *really* want to know?'

'Yes, please tell me,' I now begged as I pushed myself to recall if anything happened last night. It seemed that everything that happened between the fourth shot and this morning never found a place in my head. I had blacked out.

'You don't want to know. Even if you do, you would not be able to keep it to yourself. And I wouldn't want to get you in trouble with Avantika.'

'Shut up Malini. Just tell me.'

'If you insist,' she smiled. 'Last night—' she paused.

'Go ahead.'

'Nothing happened,' she laughed.

'Fuck you.'

She kept laughing and then suddenly stopped and said very seriously, 'Last night, you kissed three girls and none of them were Avantika.'

What? What the fuck did she just say?

'You are kidding, right?'

'No Deb,' she said, 'Look.'

Oh, no.

She fished out her digital camera from her handbag and scrolled through the photographs. In the initial photographs, everybody looked sane and we were just smiling in those pictures. No signs of kisses. As the night went on and we came to the later pictures, the hugs and the kisses became *more* intimate and scandalous. *Fuck!*

I counted. *One. Two. Three.* My mind went into multiple convulsions as I thought about the consequences. I did not even remember how any of the girls looked like. Or *who* were they! My heart sank to my feet thinking of what had transpired last night. It was right in front of my eyes! I still could not recall anything.

I started talking to myself.

She would understand, I was not in my senses. I do not even remember what happened last night. She would not accuse me. She would not leave me. What if she does? What if she doesn't believe me? What if she thinks I am lying? What if she did the same? Would I forgive her? Would I?

I felt like shit. Why did I do it!

I looked through those pictures again just to be sure. I tried to recognize those faces but I could not. Finally, a face looked familiar.

'Who's this?' I asked just to make sure.

'Me,' she said without a change in her expressions.

'This can't be true . . . I couldn't have kissed you, did I?' I said and held my head when I saw her nodding. She was serious. 'I am so screwed.'

'Listen Deb, no one remembers anything. These photographs mean nothing. Nobody has them,' she held out the screen and deleted the folder.

'But—'

'So you don't have to tell her. It was just a silly night and nobody will ever talk about it. It is as if it never happened.'

'But I know it did . . .'

I had already decided I would not tell her. I couldn't have. She had trusted me. I could have never broken that.

On our way back to the room, Malini kept telling me that it was not a big deal and I should not feel guilty about it. *You*

wouldn't even know what happened had I not told you, she said.
She had a point.

'Were you in your senses?' I asked her.

'As in?'

'I mean . . . did you know what was happening?'

'You mean if I knew I was kissing you?' she said as she lit
her cigarette. She offered me one and I refused.

'So?'

'I did. Why are you obsessing so much about it Deb?
Nobody remembers. Nobody cares . . . It was a stupid night!'

'I do. I care.'

'Stop being such a girl about it.'

'Hmm . . .'

'I have an idea . . . get sloshed again and sleep it over. What
say?' she said and dangled the bottle of vodka in front of me.

'I don't think so.'

'Why? Are you afraid this time we might go beyond kissing?'
she said, playfully.

'Umm . . . err . . .'

'Don't worry, you are not my type,' she said and poured
the drinks.

'Aren't we drinking too much?' I asked.

'I have to forget what happened too,' she said.

'You are not going to tell him?'

'No, and neither should you,' she said. '. . . and there is no
such thing as too much drinking!'

As I walked out of the airport and my eyes scanned the crowd for her, my heart was heavy with the guilt it carried. I badly wanted to see her.

'I missed you,' Avantika said as she hugged me.

'I missed you too.'

'You two make me cry,' Malini mocked. Avantika smiled at her.

'Hey man,' Mittal said, 'Welcome back! Hi Malini,' he smiled at her flirtatiously.

'Hi Ganesh,' she smiled back.

Avantika rolled her eyes. We drove back to college and I kept asking myself whether I should tell her. She was smiling. I did not want to snatch that away from her. *Stay shut*, I told myself. *Relax*, Malini told me.

As I drove to meet Shashank at Geetika's flat, Malini's words kept ringing in my head. I was being a girl. I really didn't need to tell Avantika anything. She did not need to know something that I did not even remember happened. I was not guilty of anything! I mean not in the sense she could take it. I would *never* cheat on her.

Once back in college, I narrated the incident to Shashank who listened to it with utter shock and disgust.

'Mittal would have been so proud of you,' he said after I finished.

'I haven't told him. And you don't have to tell him,' I said.

'I will not. But I think you should tell Avantika. You might fight for a few days, but things would be fine.'

'I don't want her to feel bad . . . I mean I don't even remember what happened!' I tried to defend myself.

'All these arguments are okay, but you still need to tell Avantika. If you tell her right now, she will know that you love her and you wanted to tell her. The later you tell her, the more problems it will create.'

Geetika nodded. She was quiet the whole while. She had always loved Avantika and me as a couple and was a little disappointed with me that day.

'If you want, I can talk to her,' Shashank said.

'Thank you, but I think I will do it,' I said.

'Anyway, you *really* don't remember any of the girls you kissed?' Shashank asked and I shook my head.

I left their place after a little while. Shashank gave me some notes to study for the next day. I went back to the college trying to rearrange my words.

I knocked and entered Avantika's room.

'You?' she said. 'I thought you were with Shashank and Geetika.'

I looked at her and she looked beautiful as she always did. She had just got up, her hair covered a part of her face and her eyes looked at me behind those strands of hair, full of love, hope, optimism and belief. My eyes welled up thinking if this would be the last time we would meet like this, without an iota of distrust.

'I need to tell you something,' I said, 'please don't be mad.'

She took me by my hand and made me sit down.

'I won't be,' she said.

I started from the point Malini and I reached that room in the hostel. I narrated in detail about everything that happened over the next two days. Her eyes began to wet. Her grip around my hand became loose and my hands began to tremble. Tears trickled down her cheeks. I cursed my existence. I cursed that moment of envy that made me go to Mumbai. Every tear of hers pained and made my life a little bit more miserable. By the time I finished, she sat there, chipped at her nail polish and sobbed softly.

'I am sorry. I don't deserve you, I guess,' I said.

I waited for her to say something. She just kept looking down at her hands. I felt terrible and decided that I should leave her alone. I stood up to leave when she reached out and held my hand.

'Avantika, I am really sorry—'

She did not let me complete my sentence. She stood up and hugged me as if never to leave. I do not know how much time passed as we stood there hugging. In those moments, I believed in God. I felt I had lost her. Avantika finally looked at me, held my face in her hands, and kissed me.

'Were those kisses better than this?' she asked.

'I told you I don't remember, and even if I did, it couldn't be.'

'You would compare?' she asked again.

'Never,' I said and hugged her.

We both had tears streaming down our cheeks. We hugged, kissed, and promised that we would never leave each other. I promised never to do anything *silly* thereafter and she asked me not to feel sorry about it. She forgave me so easily that it only deepened my guilt. I was dating an angel, I really was. I did not deserve her, her love or her forgiveness.

'So you did have a good time!' she mocked.

'Can you stop it now? I am feeling enough guilty already.'

'I am sorry.'

'I am sorry. Why are you being sorry?' I hugged her.

'. . . because I am attaching so much importance to something you don't have any knowledge of doing.'

'You are way too sweet, Avantika.'

'I know that, you horny bastard,' she said and winked.

'Hmm . . .'

'And what has happened to you? You are drinking too much! I asked you not to.'

'I am sorry. I will stop now. *Sure.*'

'I hope so,' she said and smiled wickedly.

We kissed and certain things followed. Whoever said, making out after a fight is not awesome was stupid! *Wait, who said it? No one?*

It was love. It is usually very stupid for guys to put up status messages on Facebook telling the world how much they loved their girls; that is usually that is reserved for the girls to do. But moments like these make you want to tell the world how much in love you are. I contemplated putting it up, but the testosterone kicked in and I decided to be a man. After all, I did not need the world to know. I only wanted her to know what she meant to me.

I kept whispering *'I love you'* into her ears until she dozed off.

You Should Never Drink With Other Women!

Avantika cried for a few days before she came to terms with it. She said she was being irrational and she said she understood how I must have passed out. Avantika had been a raging alcoholic and a drug addict during her early college days. She knew what it like was to get sloshed and carried away. She had kissed a fair deal of guys too under the influence of pills and injections!

Thank God for that!

I was leaving the cafeteria when I came across Malini sitting there. I had not talked to her for the last few days. I had just texted her to tell her that I had told Avantika everything about us. That day, she was not sitting alone there. Mittal was sitting next to her.

'Hey,' Mittal called me.

'Hi,' I acknowledged her presence with a smile.

'Hi Deb,' she said.

'Not coming for the class?' I asked them.

'Mittal is taking me out for a movie,' she said. Mittal smiled sheepishly at me.

'Oh . . . nice.'

'Why don't you come along too?' she said. Mittal vigorously shook his head to ask me to turn down the offer. When Malini told me in Mumbai that she found Mittal cute, I thought she was kidding!

'Thank you, but short attendance, can't come . . .'

'Hmm . . . okay, if you say so . . .' she said.

I took their leave and heard them laughing as I walked away from them. Mittal was on to her in a flash. *Not bad.* I wondered if Malini had told him about what happened in Mumbai. I was sure Shashank had not told him. Geetika had called me that morning and asked if everything had sorted out. She added as an afterthought that she would bury me alive if I hurt her again. I said I would do it myself if I manage to hurt her *again*.

'Where is Mittal? He is not picking up the phone? He has to report to the placement committee office at ten,' Shashank said and tried to call him again.

'I don't know. He went to watch a movie with Malini in the afternoon, haven't had a word since then.'

'Call Malini,' he said.

'Why? Is it important?'

'Obviously!' he said, pissed off.

Shashank had our passwords to our official MDI email IDs and handled everything that needed to be taken care of. That day, Mittal had received a mail from the placement committee and every mail from them was *important*. Placement committee handled the entire placement related matters of the college. These students were responsible for our placements and hence they wielded unquestionable power over other students. They were a hated lot!

I called up Malini. Mittal picked up the call.

'Hey.'

'Hey.'

'Where are you?' I asked him.

'I am at a friend's flat,' he said. *Flat? What were they doing there?*

I handed over the phone to Shashank who blasted him for ignoring mails from the placement committee!

It was a strange feeling to think Malini was up to something with Mittal. I could not put a finger on why it felt a little quirky. I let the feeling pass. It took him an hour to reach the college and I was a little restless until they reached. I felt guilty that I actually *cared* about these two being together. I should *not* have!

'When did I have to report?' he asked as he approached us. Malini followed closely behind.

Shashank asked Mittal not to act fresh with the *placecom* guys! They were a bunch of arrogant, high-nosed people, and Shashank told Mittal what pretext he should give them. Mittal nodded and went inside the office. Shashank left to meet Geetika soon after.

'How was the movie?'

'We didn't watch it,' Malini said.

'Aha,' I smirked. 'What did you do then?'

'Oh please. Nothing happened,' she blew me off.

'I never said *anything* happened.'

'But you *meant* that.'

'I didn't,' I said.

'Don't give me those jealous boyfriend looks,' she said. 'Anyway, why have they called him?'

'No idea. And I gave you no looks!'

We waited for a couple of minutes before he came out of the room with his head hung low and a dead expression across her face. Something had gone wrong.

'What's the matter?' Malini asked him. He looked at us with dead eyes and shoulders hung. He was never usually sad. I wondered what had happened.

'I got *PLACED!*'

He shrieked aloud and hugged me. My bones were crushed in his grip and I could hardly fathom what Malini went through after he hugged her equally hard. We were immensely happy for him. Jobs were *why* we were there! It was a great relief for him. It would have been for anyone. We called up Shashank and Avantika and told them about the offer and they were awesomely excited for him.

'Where are you taking us tonight?' Avantika asked as she reached the canteen within a few minutes.

'Today?'

'Why? What's the problem with today?' she asked.

'Shashank isn't here,' Mittal said.

'You can take him out some time else . . . Do not lose *this* moment!' she argued.

'Where do you want to go?'

We finalized on a new unaffordable nightclub near MDI that we had never thought we would go to. Mittal had convinced Malini to come along! Malini could not say no.

While he was at it, I could see Avantika shifting in her place. She did not look too comfortable with Malini tagging along but she could not have said anything.

That night, it was going to be the four of *us!*

'It is fucking ten thirty man,' Mittal said.

'*Girls!*'

'Call Avantika . . . Malini isn't picking up.'

I called up Avantika and she did not pick up either. The last time she had picked up, she had said she would be ready in five minutes. It had been half an hour since then. We waited for another fifteen minutes when these two showed up. And I am not kidding when I say that every eye ball in the college cafeteria turned towards them as they sashayed towards us in their short dresses, radiant faces and beautiful hair.

Avantika wore a flaming red off shoulder dress that ended a few inches above her knees. Her bright red stilettos made her look almost as tall as me. She had let her hair open and she flashed a big enrapturing smile as her eyes met mine. Her eyes never looked as bigger and as captivating as they looked then. She had never looked more beautiful. I do not know how many *times* I had said this to her in the last three years.

Somehow, Avantika just managed to look more beautiful than the last time I used to see her dressed up for some special occasion.

'Stop staring, let's go,' she winked.

'You just kill me *every* time.'

'I know,' she smiled.

She was a work of art. It was only later that I saw what Malini wore—a *little* black dress! It was *little!* She was all shiny legs that day. A little bit of cleavage thrown in too. And yeah, I have to admit, she looked steaming hot.

Avantika—*the quintessential beauty* Vs. Malini—*the hot temptress!*

We were certainly not complaining. We just felt awesomely lucky to be around such great looking women.

'Let's go?' Mittal said as he put the car in gear.

'I love what you are wearing,' Malini said.

'Thank you. You look pretty! Only if I were not straight . . .' Avantika answered. They both laughed out and hugged. To see two extremely hot women touch each other is such a remarkable sight. No wonder good old *girl-on-girl* action porn always finds space in every guy's hidden folders!

'I am sure MDI has never seen such beautiful things before,' Mittal said to me.

The '*things*' comment didn't go down too well with the ladies in the back seat. They said we were treating them as pieces of meat! We were not to blame. They looked hot as if they came straight out of magazines that guys take to their washrooms for a little time *alone*.

Mittal kept the mood chirpy until we reached there, while I was just busy looking at Avantika . . . and sometimes at Malini. *Innocent* glances at those never-ending legs and the few inches of cleavage that she flaunted.

It took us just over an hour to get there. We parked the car and got down from it.

'It's very flattering, but will you stop staring?' Avantika winked and walked ahead of me. Her ass was . . . umm . . . very grab*able!* Malini nudged me from behind, 'She does look awesome, doesn't she?'

I nodded and added, 'So do you.' She smiled.

We entered the gates and immediately knew why this place was so highly rated. The huge dance floor was lit up in maze of laser lights of a million different colours. The place stunk of money, brats and expensive alcohol. There were hot people making out everywhere! Total *sex*pots.

'Here we are!' Mittal shouted out to our deaf ears.

'Let's get *drunk!*' Malini joined in. Avantika shouted out her approval. I just looked at Avantika and smiled. It reminded me of Goa. The last time we got drunk. *Together.*

'What will you guys have?' Malini asked all of us as she pushed and shoved her way to the counter.

We all ordered shots for us. Avantika was the designated driver for the night so she stayed away from anything.

'Can we dance? Or you need to be more drunk?' Avantika asked me, a little miffed at my decision to drink that day. I could already see her feet moving even while she was sitting. She had learnt an impressive array of dances from to salsa to *bachata* to names that I could not even pronounce!

'Just one more,' I shouted back. 'Or maybe two!'

One more went on until I was seven shots down. Or was it eight? I had started to grope or feel her up but she pulled me on to the dance floor. We made our way past half-naked girls who moved their asses and hips in the most provocative ways possible. Soon, Avantika was one of them. Only better, sexier and hotter!

She held me by the neck and pulled me into her as we grappled for space on the floor. She let her tongue run over my ears as her hands grabbed me by my hair. I found my hand was on her leg, which was by then wrapped around my waist and pushed me further in to her. I found my other hand around her swaying waist, as her body gyrated against me. Her ass swayed and I did with it. I felt my hands going all over her and her hands going all over me. In those moments, she was stronger than I was! It almost felt like nobody was watching us, as she turned and pulled me, kissed me, and her tongue explored every bit of me. She moved like I had never seen her move before. She left me panting and wanting for more when we walked off the dance floor.

'What happened?' I asked her in my slurred speech as I followed her off the dance floor.

'Let's keep *something* for the night, shall we?'

'As you say.'

She excused herself for a little girl time and left for the washroom as I glugged down the rest of my drink that I left on the table. It had gotten warm, but it had no taste, not to me. I looked at the watch. It had been more than an hour that we had been dancing and it hardly felt like it. I ordered another drink and looked around for the rest of the two. I browsed my eyes through scores of little black dresses but I could not find hers!

Suddenly, I found in one corner, Malini! She sat alone, cross-legged, her perfectly sculpted legs shining. The jogs around the campus had really shown effect. She never looked hotter. I went up to her, flopped on the couch next to her, and suppressed an urge to run my fingers over her naked thighs. How much you drink is directly proportional to how horny you are!

'Where is he?'

'He?' she asked. Her eyes were rolling up. She was definitely drunk. 'Oh . . . he has just gone for a smoke.'

'You didn't go, you Toronto return babe?' I mocked.

Sense of humour really goes for a toss when you are drunk. Nevertheless, we just cannot shut up, can we?

'No, I am just a little too drunk,' she said and put both her hands around my neck.

'Yes. You seem so,' I said, my head still spinning.

'And you are so sweet,' she said, her eyes losing focus, and closing.

'Thank you.'

She leaned further into me and her hands went around me. 'You are such a nice guy,' she said, touched my nose with her finger and tapped it.

'You are not all that bad either.'

She hugged me again. I felt her pushing her body against mine. Closer and closer still. Her hands held my face and pulled it closer to hers. Her face hovered near mine and her breath warmed up mine as if wafted from her parted lips to mine. I felt her lips brush against mine. Her perfume overwhelmed my nostrils. She looked deep into my eyes with those limpid wet eyes of hers and asked me to come closer. Her lips enveloped mine. Mine hers. I felt the wetness on my lips. I felt her on mine.

'Deb?' I heard, amidst all the noise. I looked up.

Avantika!

The Break

We had not spoken since an hour. She stood by the door and I sat on the bed. I could hear the silent sobs. She did not look at me once and it was killing me from inside. I did not know what to say. I sat there rewinding repeatedly as to what happened and why I let it happen. I was praying she would say something and not stand there and cry. It was getting unbearable and I just wanted to hug her and say that I was *sorry.* But sorry? *Again?* I could only imagine what she must be going through.

I had kissed the same girl, twice in fifteen days. This time I was not even drunk. I knew exactly what was happening there in the nightclub.

This time I did not even know what to say. I needed to look into myself this time before talking to Avantika. *What did I just do? Why did I kiss Malini?* I wanted these answers for myself before I could say anything to Avantika. Was it a mistake? *Twice?* I was scared. I had no idea of what was happening to me.

'Deb,' she said as steeled her voice. The gravity in her voice shook me.

'Yes,' my voice trembled.

'You should go now.'

'What?' I said. I should go? Like forever? Was that what she meant? I hoped not. I did not move. I did not want to. *What had I done?*

'You should leave,' she said, 'Just go.'

'But—' I said and I had nothing to say.

'Please don't say anything, just go Deb.'

I left the room, my eyes stuck at her until she closed the door. I saw those eyes, stricken and filled with tears. I walked through the corridors, my head hung low and tears streaked down my streaks.

'Just go Deb.'

Her words kept ringing through my head. I felt sick in the pit of my stomach .I went to my room and logged into Gmail. She pinged me as soon as I was online.

>**Avantika:** *Why, Deb? Why?'*
>
>**Me:** *I am sorry Avantika, I don't know how it happened. I am really sorry. I love you. You know I do. Don't you?☹*
>
>**Avantika:** *Whatever I saw today makes me doubt everything Deb. You shared a room with her for two nights. God knows now what happened then?*
>
>**Me:** *For the sake of everything we shared over the last few years, please believe me. I am not lying. I will never lie to you. She just came on to me.*
>
>**Avantika:** *Don't give me that. I saw you. Don't just put it on her.*
>
>**Me:** *I am sorry Avantika. I know it is hard to trust me, but please baby, I love you, and I love you more than anything in this world. Please, you know that.*
>
>**Avantika:** *But it is not good enough. How do I forget what*

I saw? I was right there Deb, right there! Would you have accepted it?

Me: *I am sorry.*

Avantika: *I want to forgive you. I really do. But I really don't know what to do.*

Me: *Avantika don't do this.*

Avantika: *I just think we should stay away for a little time.*

Me: *Please don't? I wouldn't be able to take it. Please, don't do this to me.*

Avantika: *Let me figure out things. Give me some time. Let's take a break.*

Me: *Are you leaving me?*

I had tears in my eyes as I wrote this.

Avantika: *I never said that. I just want to be alone for a little while. And probably you need to get a few things straight too. Take this time to do it.*

Me: *Baby, don't do this. Please, let me come to you. I am sorry. Please.*

Avantika: *Deb, please. All I am asking from you, please, don't contact me for a few days. Please. I love you Deb, I always will, but please?*

Me: *How long, baby?*

Avantika: *I will tell you. Bye baby. Take care.*

I was crying now. I was frantic, shaking. *She cannot do that me*, I thought. But she could. She just did.

Me: *Bye.*

She went offline as soon as I wrote this. And I went crazy. I sent off-liners and she did not reply. I sent a zillion mails asking for forgiveness. I wrote to her to tell her how much she meant to me and how much I hated myself for what I had done. She did not reply. I called her, but she cut the phone every time and messaged me not to call her.

Her message read:

> Love you, Deb. But I need some time alone. Please give me that. I trust you. Your love. Just let me be with myself for a few days. Please don't message and call me to make it worse. Please baby.

I could only send an 'okay' to her.

I was choking on my own tears, crying like a girl, howling. I felt angry and disgusted at myself and at Malini. I wanted to call up Shashank but I felt ashamed. I had no argument this time. This time, I had screwed up bad. I re-read the chat a million times, my eyes never left Google talk list to see if she unblocks me. She did not. The room came onto bite me. I dialled her number at least a hundred times and cut it. I wrote a long message telling her how much I wanted her back and how I would make things right and sent it over, but she did not reply!

I sent a few more.

> 'Please forgive me, baby. I love you, don't do this to me, to yourself. I want you around. I know I have been terrible, but I love you baby. Please come back. Please baby . . . I don't even like her. I don't know how it happened. Swear on you. Swear on anyone, I was just drunk, and in Mumbai, I didn't even know what happened. I am sorry baby. Please don't do this to me. I will do what you want baby, just talk to me once? Just once? Please? Please?'

This time I had absolutely no excuse. The worst part was— I did not even have an answer for myself. What I did was a stupid, horny mistake . . . but *why?* I knew it was wrong, but why did I do it! I wish I could undo the last twelve hours. I wished I had never known Malini.

I lost count of how many such messages I sent that night.

Not one reply came. Every time the phone beeped, my heart rate fastened only to be dampened for it would not be her. The calls went unanswered. I waited for the morning class where I would get to see her again. Time came to a standstill; every minute seemed like an hour, laborious and torturous. I just told myself that things would be fine the next day. I closed my eyes, and hoped that when I will wake up, it will be all gone. Like a bad dream. I consoled myself that she would read all the messages and feel for me.

I reached the class five minutes early and did not take any seat. I waited for her to come so I could sit next to her. Time passed and she did not come. The professor entered the class and she was still nowhere to be seen. I wondered if she was okay. I took the seat where we usually used to sit. After five minutes, she entered the class. One innocent smile with a believable pretext is all it took her to get attendance. It looked like she didn't sleep too that night. She took the first row seat.

I messaged her. She did not seem to bring her phone out of her handbag like she always did. Maybe she did not get it to class. I passed on a note to her. She read it, crumpled it. She looked behind and her eyes seemed to say, *Please leave me alone*.

She could still say a million words with just one look. I never won any of those eye conversations. The class crawled to its finish and Avantika left the class in a hurry. I walked behind her, but clearly, she did not want to talk to me. Or even look at me. I felt disgusted with myself for what I did to her. She entered the girls' hostel and I stood there hoping she would at least look back once and acknowledge my presence. She did not and I trudged back to the room. I sent her a few more messages hoping she would check her phone messages once she gets back to her room.

I signed into Google talk, with the only hope that she would have unblocked me. She surprisingly had. Never had I been more relived or happy to see her name on that list. *Was the break over?* I asked myself. She pinged.

Avantika : *What if I had done the same with Kabir?*

Me : *Don't say that baby.*

Avantika : *I am sorry. Give me some time Deb. I will be fine. I miss you. Bye.*

She signed off. Or blocked me again. I read the conversation repeatedly. The first sentence was as hurting as the last one was comforting. She missed me and I smiled. I read it again and I smiled again. I lay down on the bed saying the last sentence to myself all the time. I told myself that it would be over soon. I closed my eyes and tried to catch up on some sleep between the two classes.

In an hour that I tried to sleep, I woke up more than ten times to see if she had unblocked me, but she had not. I rushed to the class as soon as it was time.

'Still fighting?' Mittal asked.

'She is not talking to me.'

'It will be fine. Malini asked me tell you that she was sorry,' he said and for the first time, Mittal sounded sorry.

I noticed that Malini was not in the class. *Slut,* I said to myself. Was it *really* her fault?

Mittal told me Malini was not picking his calls and had asked him to fuck off. *Guilt,* I figured. I had gotten used to the feeling in the past few days. It kills you and empties you from the inside. The class ended and Avantika walked out of the class without even looking at me once. It was as if I was alone in the world!

Suddenly, life had gone so empty. I called up Shashank, but he was going out of the town with Geetika for a couple of days. I dragged my feet to the room and lay down on the bed. My phone lay besides me. It was not ringing. She was not calling every few minutes with her calls and messages. How I wished she had something to call me for: some assignment, some extra class, something! Anything!

Everything in the room reminded me of her. I fiddled with my phone and called her a few times. But the same result, she didn't pick up. I left my room, as it got hard for me to stay there any longer. It did not help much. I walked around the campus and saw her everywhere. Couples were sitting around, talking about the next quiz, the placement season, CGPAs. Memories of Avantika flooded my mind. I was choking. The pain was getting harder to live with every moment. She would come back; it is just a break, I told myself.

How could I be such a big asshole?

I walked past a bench on which we often spent our nights talking about the past that we had seen and the future that lay in front of us. I sat there and hoped the pain would get a little lesser. She would miss me and come to that bench too, I thought. Music gave me company, all our favourite songs filled up my ears as I sat there for hours. She did not come. Suddenly, I saw her running in front me. I heard *her* crying.

Malini.

The jog. Those legs. Those sinful legs. *Slut*, I thought. I was one too.

I Just Needed Someone to Talk to

Did Malini want to seduce me? *I did not know.* Was I even worth seducing? *I did not know.* Did I ever think of kissing her? *No.* Did I ever think about the kiss? *No.*

Then why?

It had been a week and every evening I had seen her jog past that bench. Sometimes, she had tears in her eyes. There were times that I had thought of calling out her name and talking to her. She had not talked to anybody in a week.

Finally, I called out her name. She stopped and we stood there looking at each other for quite some time. I kissed her? I could not have! I did *not* love her, I loved Avantika . . . how could I? I do not know what she was thinking but my mind battled with the thought of abusing her for screwing me up so bad.

'You wouldn't want to talk to me,' she cried aloud.

'I shouldn't,' I shouted back. She started walking away, still crying.

'Malini!' I shouted out again. 'Maybe I should.'

'Maybe you should not,' she wailed out.

It had been one hour on that bench and we had still not exchanged a word. She fiddled with her earphones. A tear or two trickled down her cheek occasionally. I could not care less. I just sat there and tried to figure out just one answer . . . why Deb? Why did I kiss her? It became clear to me that it was just the alcohol. I had no feelings for her whatsoever.

'I am sorry,' she said, breaking the silence.

'Hmm . . .'

'I really didn't mean to . . .'

'I know . . .'

'I am such a whore,' she said.

My thoughts had always wandered in that direction, but I was *equally* at fault. I had spent hours thinking about what made me do what I did, and nothing seemed to make sense.

'I am sorry for ruining it,' she said.

'*Nothing* is ruined. She will come back. I will make her come back.'

'You can't do that if you sit next to me,' she said.

'Hmm . . .'

'I should go.'

'Maybe.'

She shook my hand, wished me luck and walked away. And suddenly in a moment, I had no one to talk to again.

The nights were even harder. The darker it got the more painful it became. I closed my diary, the repository of all the beautiful things I had shared with her: the big fights, the big loves, the big surprises, the birthdays and the anniversaries! Everything!

The pain got unbearable. It was as if somebody was stabbing me repeatedly and those stabs never missed the heart. I became restless, wanted to walk up to her room and bang on her door. But all she wanted was a few days alone. I took a deep breath and told myself that everything would be fine. Maybe I was just obsessing. I had never missed her so much.

'It will be fine man,' Shashank said, his voice cracking.

I could hear Geetika behind shouting at him for something. They had gone off to Shimla for the weekend. Amid the hills with a chill in the air, a warm quilt and your loved one in your arms; Shashank had it all. I too had all that. I lost it. I cut the phone and apologized for disturbing him. My mind was now stuck there. Every trip that Avantika and I had gone to flashed in front of my eyes.

Kasauli. Rishikesh. Goa. Mumbai. The long talks on the balconies, the early morning bed teas, the late night snuggles, the morning showers, the 'cancel-all-plans-and-stay-here' looks, the pecks, the packing and the unpacking. It all came right in front of my eyes. I slept peacefully that day, without a worry, without a frown, with a lot of love in my heart, images of her in my eyes and the hope that things will be fine the next day.

The days were not getting any better. I obsessed about tracking every movement of hers, from her room to the class, from the library to the mess, from the mess to the classroom . . . I was going crazy. My only consolation was to see her crying occasionally. It gave me a glimmer of hope that she missed me in her life and that she wanted me back as much I wanted her.

It had been two weeks now. There was nothing more comforting than watching her every day.

Once in a few days, I used to bombard her with calls, messages and mails and all she did was to tell me sweetly that she needed time and she still loved me. I could never say anything beyond it.

Over the last few days, all the study groups had started working on their assignments, which meant Avantika was spending a lot of time with her group and Kabir. To see her with Kabir pained me. I put myself in her place and imagined what it must be like for her to see me with Malini *that* day.

Anyway, the few hours that I spent on the bench became a regular affair. I used to sit there and wait for Avantika to come. She never did but I saw Malini every day on her evening jog with a dead look on her face and tears in her eyes. I could see her pick up pace as she reached near the bench. We avoided eye contact. Sometimes I thought of calling out her name, but then used to decide otherwise.

'Get over her!' Mittal told me.

'Mittal, it's just a break.'

'That is exactly what I am trying to tell you. She *will* come back. Just wait for her, why do you have to follow her around!'

'I am not following her around.'

'You are . . . if you had it your way you would have gone to the movie hall today and waited till the movie got over,' he said.

'Movie hall?' I asked, a little puzzled.

'What? *They* have gone for a movie right?'

'Who? They?'

'Kabir and Avantika.'

'What?' I said as my whole body combusted into flames instantaneously.

Shashank who had been quietly working on a case study all this time, now spoke up, 'Stop kidding Mittal.'

I saw a few uncomfortable looks exchanged between the two of them. Shashank knew *too*. They had gone for a movie and it seemed I was the *last* one to know. Apparently, her whole study group had planned to watch a movie but people had dropped out. I left the room, despite the repeated pleas of Mittal and Shashank to relax. I went to my room and checked the newspaper to see the places where the movie played. A hell lot of places; there was no way I could have told where they had gone.

Three long hours. And maybe a little after that too. My heart pounded as my eyes followed the seconds' hands on my watch turn. I left my room and headed for the MDI gate. I walked around in circles, sat, drank cups of coffee, and desperately tried to make time go faster. My eyes were stuck on the approach road to MDI and I looked for his car. I had been waiting since four hours for them to come back from that wretched movie!

DL 9CB 0677

I saw both of them sitting in the car. Just the two of them as the car whizzed past me. Avantika was smiling. The car did *not* enter the MDI gate. It went straight ahead. *Where the fuck are they going now?*

She switched off the phone after the twentieth call. It was

eight in the night.

What are they doing? Seven hours together? What are they talking about? What the fuck are they up to?

All these questions filled up my head as I trudged back inside the campus after waiting for hours on that dusty street for them to come back. Kabir's phone was not working either. I was going crazy! What the fuck were they doing outside college! I imagined a lot of things . . . unpleasant things. *I will forgive her,* I told myself.

Was he making her laugh? Was he touching her? Was he telling her how beautiful she looked?

My head started to pain and my heart started sinking. I slumped down on the bench. And waited.

For Avantika. For Malini.

'What's the matter?' she asked. She was not crying that day.

'Nothing.'

A few minutes of silence passed between us. 'She is out with Kabir today,' I said, not looking at her.

'I know. I saw them leave the campus,' she said. 'Don't think *too* much.'

'I wish.'

'You want to talk?' she asked me.

'Hmm . . .'

'I am stinking right now, so let me just come back in five,' she said. 'And don't let that smile go off your face while I am away.'

I didn't know what smile she was talking about. I lost count of the days since I smiled last. She walked away leaving me on that bench alone, and in a mélange of thoughts in my mind of Avantika, Malini and that bastard—Kabir.

I had once asked Avantika when we had started going out that what she would think of the girl who would make me cheat on her. Avantika said she would not blame the girl. *Why shouldn't she have her share of fun?* But I blamed Kabir. He knew everything about the two us, but he was still trying to charm his way into her life.

'Did you ask her how the movie was?' Malini said as she walked up to me.

'That's not funny.'

'No, it isn't,' she said as she lit up the cigarette. 'Want one?'

'No, thank you.'

'Want to talk about what happened?' she said.

'I don't know. She just wanted a break for a little while. It has been more than fifteen days now. Now, this Kabir issue, it is totally freaking me out.'

'It's just a phase. It will go away. You want me to talk to her?' she said.

'No, it is fine.'

'Please let me do something for you. The guilt is killing me. And it wouldn't go until I see you both together,' she said and I saw those tears again in her eyes.

'We will be together,' I said. It was more of a wish than a belief.

'I hope so.'

'Anyway, what is on with your guy? Did you tell him?'

'There is nothing to talk about him,' her voice took solemn tone. 'And I don't want to talk about him.'

'Hmm . . .'

I wished she would say something. Something that would

tell me that my life sucked lesser than hers did.

'He cheated on me,' she said after a long pause. *Thank God! It sucked.*

'Oh . . .' I said. 'So used me to get back at him?'

'I didn't tell him about us,' she said. 'And I didn't use you. I didn't want to hurt him or exact revenge. I was just angry and drunk that day. And it happened . . . I am sorry.'

'Don't be.'

'I am. I really didn't intend to *use* you.'

'I was just thinking you did it to me because you thought I was hot . . .' I joked. Probably the first time in the last fifteen days I had tried my hand at humour. I smiled at my own joke.

'You are irresistible,' she mocked. 'Don't you see all the girls lining up?'

'Blah.'

Malini never let go of her sarcasm, no matter what. And in some ways, it was endearing. And in many other ways, irritating.

'Avantika wouldn't like it if she knows that you were with me.'

'She is out with Kabir, isn't she?'

'Revenge won't help you win her back,' she said.

'Hmm. It's not revenge. Shashank and Mittal are both sceptical about the way I am reacting to the whole situation, so I really can't talk to them. You seem to be the only option. And I don't want to tell anyone else about it.'

'I don't care if everyone knows,' she said coldly.

'I am sorry if that hurt.'

'It didn't. I seriously don't give a fuck,' she puffed on her cigarette. She often reminded me of the Avantika that *used* to be: the Avantika who had gone to rehabilitation to kick her habits. The Avantika I had never seen, but heard stories about. A lot of stories. More nasty than nice.

Silence hung over.

As I walked back to the cafeteria that night I saw Avantika walking towards the library. She was back after her *long* date with Kabir. Our eyes shared a brief awkward moment. I tried to ask a million questions and her eyes gave no answer. I looked around the boys' hostel to see where Kabir was. He was sleeping and I wanted to strangulate him with his pillow. I decided against it . . . *Why shouldn't he have his share of fun?*

I went back to the room and opened the research methodology book with the hope of doing something constructive, but that was something difficult to do even when I had nothing on my mind. I could not concentrate after a few minutes. I fiddled with the phone scrolling between Avantika's number and Malini's. I called up Avantika. She rejected my call and sent me a message.

What? Everything okay.

I messaged her back.

Was worried about you. Where were you the whole day?

Her reply came after a few minutes.

Was busy.

Those messages blew my head off. She was not busy; she was out for a movie with him! I called up Malini, almost on a reflex.

'Hey,' she said.

'What are you doing?' I asked her.

'You seem to be angry.'

'That is because I am,' I said. 'See you at the canteen.'

I cut the phone.

A few minutes later, we were walking towards the canteen nearest to the library.

'Where is Avantika?' she asked as soon as she met me.

'Library,' I said.

She tried hard to keep up pace with me as I walked towards the canteen. Malini put her hand on the shoulder in order to tell me to take it easy. Her touch was awkward and she withdrew her hand. As we walked to the canteen, quite a few eye balls had turned towards us. I was accustomed to it now, because no guy in the college would go past Avantika and would not glare. This time, I could see surprise in their eyes.

Malini and Deb?

It did not matter though. We ordered noodles and took our seats at the open-air canteen. My eyes were firmly stuck at the approach way to the library. I slurped noodles in.

'So how long do we plan to sit here and look there?' she said and laughed out. 'You are so hopelessly in love with her, aren't you?'

'I am just okayishly in love,' I said, trying not to sound sissy. 'I am sorry.'

'Sorry? Sorry for what?'

'. . . for dragging you here late at night for nothing at all.'

'I am the very reason you are here. You needn't be sorry,' she said.

I could do nothing but smile. We sat there for another half an hour or so, and just got bored of just sitting there. There was no sign of Avantika.

'Let' go,' I said.

'Where? Library?' she asked.

'No. Back.'

'As you say,' she said and I paid the canteen guy.

As I walked past the library, I saw her studying. Nothing had changed. She still made my heart skip a couple of beats whenever I looked at her. Right across the table . . . it was him, Kabir.

Kabir?

Wasn't he in his hostel room a while ago? I walked away and felt a pat from Malini. Her eyes seemed to say, everything would be fine. I smiled.

Over the next few days, I spotted Kabir and Avantika everywhere. Canteen. Class. Library (mostly!).

I was sure she spotted me too. With Malini. I *wanted* her to. It sure would be painful for her but there was no reaction from her side. Not even one sign of discomfort. The fact that she did not care was hurting me more than the fact that she was all over the college with Kabir.

Did she move on?

I often argued with myself that I should not be around Malini, but every time I saw Avantika with Kabir, I just had to call Malini up. If it was hard for her, it was hard for me too. I needed someone too. Malini was my only way out of depression.

'What is love to you?' Malini asked me that day. We had gone out to a movie. Shashank had told me that he had seen Kabir and Avantika hanging together at a mall in Vasant Kunj.

'Hmm . . . I don't know.'

'Don't be so lame,' she said as we stood in line for popcorn.

'I can't put it in words.'

'Try to. We are in a management course, this is what we should be good at,' she smiled.

'Hmm . . . is it . . . Let me try.'

'Please do,' she said.

'Love? It isn't a feeling, it's *her*. I can only think of her when I think about love. She is pretty much my definition for it. I mean she taught me what it was. She made me feel what it was. She made me do all the crazy things that I did for her, things that we did together, things that she did for me. Over the last three years, she has been *love* for me! She still is . . . always will be. I had once heard in a movie, the power of a relationship lies with the one who cares less. Before Avantika came around, I had always been powerful, cared less and always protected myself from getting hurt! However, when Avantika came, everything changed. She changed me . . .' I paused. 'We should go in . . .'

The movie resumed and people rushed in.

'We should stay. This is better,' she took my hand and pulled me to the food court. 'Continue,' she said as she sipped her cold coffee.

'Continue?'

'Whatever you were saying about love . . . and her,' she said and looked straight onto me.

'I said what I had to. I just love her. I don't know what love is, or how it is supposed to be, but she is the closest I will ever get to it.'

'She changed you, you said. So what were you? A player . . . because you don't look like one,' she laughed aloud.

'Whatever.'

'Aww . . . but you do look cute, when you get all lovey-dovey and stuff. No wonder she adores you.'

'Thank you, but nowadays, she adores that son of a bitch.'

She laughed. 'C'mon. Don't be such a kid. She will come back.'

'I know. Somehow, I fear she will not. I cheated on her and now, I am sitting with the same girl I cheated on her with, while she is on a break. And before you say anything . . . I didn't say that to make you feel guilty again.'

A few seconds of silence hung over us after which she spoke, 'Samarth got drunk and made out twice with two different girls in three days. It is acceptable, as long the girlfriend doesn't get to know. But I do know now.'

'What did you do?'

'Nothing.'

'Hurt?' I asked. *Stupid question.*

'Yes. But who do I blame? I am not the prettiest girl in his life. He is there. One and half years without me, he still calls me every day, mails me, says he loves me and we still are not together. He is a guy after all. He needs all that. What can I do?'

'Hmm . . .'

'But love is different from lust, isn't it?'

'Is it?' I asked.

'I mean even if he makes out with someone else, he can still be in love with me, right?' Her questions made me uncomfortable.

'Yes. Probably.'

Malini told me everything about her relationship with Samarth. For the first time in the month or two I had known her, I saw the sarcasm melt away. I saw the love struck side of hers. She blushed like a little schoolgirl while she narrated about her dates with Samarth. Love *changes* everybody.

No matter how much she tried to show how tough and unnerved she was from the outside, but from the inside, she was softer and mushier than a melted ice cream scoop.

That day, my whole perception about her changed. She was just another girl trying to mend her broken heart. Because guys, be it Toronto or Delhi, are assholes!

'Where were you?' Shashank asked.

'With Malini. Where else!' Mittal said. 'I told you that you will get over Avantika! Malini isn't a bad choice, Deb.'

Shashank and I looked at him until he shut up. I cannot recall the last time Mittal had not thought from his dick. I did not blame him though; he reminded me of an *old* me, with a little more hormones raging in his veins and his pants.

'What's going on with Malini?' Shashank asked. As usual, he was very serious. It seemed as if it was his responsibility to take care that I didn't screw up anything I had with Avantika.

'Nothing,' I said.

'He wants to bang her,' Mittal said.

'. . . I have to keep myself occupied,' I said.

'Deb needs to keep his dick occupied,' Mittal said.

'Mittal, will you please shut the fuck up?' Shashank said angrily.

'If you say so . . . but just remember, it is all about sex!' he said and moved out. We could hear a *hello* in the background. He was on the phone again.

Shashank continued, 'Now, what is the matter? Tell me. Why Malini? Trying to make her jealous?'

'Part of it, yes.'

'You will make it worse.'

'It makes my days easier,' I said. 'Besides, she is with Kabir.'

'You *think* so?'

'Yes.'

'You are a fool if you think that,' he said. 'Think about her for once.'

I did not want to talk about it. It was already hard enough not to think about her. I was sick of everyone giving me love advice. I did not want to talk any further and I told him that. He said I could go to him whenever I needed him and we moved on to more other topics.

Shashank went on to reprimand me for not attending the Organizational Behaviour classes. The professor took class participation seriously and gave a hard time to whoever missed his classes. Shashank said I had exhausted all my allowed leaves and I should go prepared to his next class. As always, he had marked whatever I needed to study for the next class.

I browsed through the chapter. Nothing really made sense so I crammed it all up. So did Mittal, who left the course midway citing that the professor would call me for the presentation, not him. The professor was unusually hard on absentees.

A Smile Changes It All

Subir Verma was probably the smartest professor in MDI. But that wasn't what he was known for! He was known for his mercurial temper, and many students had bore the brunt of it. He was known to dock peoples' placements on his whims. Other than that, he was a cool guy. I just wished that it were one of his good mood days.

My hopes were dashed when he banged the door shut from inside even though he was a few minutes before time. He took the attendance and his eyes stayed for more than a few seconds on me. *He would choose me*, I thought. He had spotted my absence in class as Shashank had said he would.

'Deb, to the board,' he said as he walked up the stairs of the class. 'Show me the slides.'

I put the pen drive in and clicked on the icon. The slides Shashank had prepared for me showed up on the projector screen.

'Start,' he said.

'. . . the companies were named Acme and Omega, where Acme retained the original management style . . .' I started reading from the slides.

'What? What did you just say?' he bellowed.

'Sir . . . original . . . original management . . .'

'Sixth semester . . . and this is what you say . . . engineering background, isn't it?' he asked.

'Yes sir, mechanical engineer . . .'

He resumed the shouting, 'That's why the GARBAGE . . . Just because you have paid the fees does not mean I am obliged to listen to your garbage and suffer you. Give me the goddamned word for the organization. For Acme and for Omega! NOW!'

'Sir, Omega was a flat organization, whereas Acme was a tall organization with more hierarchy . . .'

'What kind of class am I holding here? Is this an English class or an organizational behaviour class . . . you are going to be a God darn manager Deb . . . use words like decentralization, differentiation . . . DO IT . . .'

'Sir, Acme is more horizontally differentiated . . . Omega is not, but the power is more decentralized . . .' I spoke for a few minutes and sprinkled as much jargon as I could. It didn't work.

'What crap are you talking Deb?' he shouted out again. 'Give me that word. Or you get a minus ten in class participation. NOW.'

He was certainly not kidding. He had done that before and it was normal for him to fuck up anyone's grade.

'Leave the class if you don't know. Leave the class right now!'

Minus ten, plus a grade dock if I left the class would have meant a death knell for my grade in that subject. I stood there and stared blankly at the professor. With every second I could see my grades slipping. *A-*, *A*, *B-*, *B* . . . nope, definitely a *D-*

! I was screwed.

He shouted once. Twice. And again. I was battling with the thought of either standing there like a dumbass and hope he would cool down, or move out and avoid angering him further. I shifted the gaze and started looking down the podium, dejected.

'Did you not hear me? Give me the terms, or get out of the class.'

I looked up and saw Avantika staring right at from three benches away from me. She was trying to tell me something. She mouthed something, her lips moved. I followed her lips . . . as I had done so many times in the past.

'Sir . . . Oorganic . . . and . . . m . . . ee . . .' I was not sure. She showed me a *thumbs-up*. I followed her lips even closely.

'Mechanistic . . . ?' I said, this time a lot more confident. Avantika was with me. *Right there.* She smiled. I felt students sighing. They were actually wishing that I got the word! A sadistic professor unites classmates like nothing else does.

'FINALLY . . . Right! Go back to your seat. Kanika . . . to the board.'

I went to my seat, smiling and slightly relieved. I looked at Avantika but she was looking in her book. I was smiling. First contact in a month. I was smiling the hardest I had ever smiled.

'Avantika?' Shashank whispered in my ear.

'Yes.' We both smiled at each other.

'It was Avantika, right?' Malini asked as we sat down for lunch.

'Yes.'

'So, you are going to talk to her?' She said as she offered me a *papad*.

'Yes.'

'When? Do it now!' she said. She was visibly excited.

'I will call her tonight.'

Now that she had sort of responded, I was at ease. At least I was not getting paranoid now. Things would be fine now. After all, she smiled at me in the class, I said to myself. Sooner or later. Better sooner than later.

It was my tenth call to her that night and there was still no answer. All that good feeling that came out from what had happened earlier in the class vanished. I was not really feeling that great anymore. Maybe what happened in the class was just out of pity of seeing me stand there and getting slaughtered by a Hitler*esque* professor. I went online and she was not even there. I paced around the room, called up Malini who said what everyone said. *Things will be fine.* But when?

My question still went unanswered. A question that I had asked myself a million times. I sat down on the corner of the bed with the phone in my hand. I scrolled through all the pictures we had clicked together. We were so fucking happy. Why did all this had to happen?

I felt a few tears trickle down. It seemed so pointless that I was killing myself over someone who did not even care what was happening to me. I flipped open the laptop and logged onto Youtube to take my mind off her. There was a knock on the door. I wiped off the dried streaks of tears and switched on the lights. I got the door . . . .And the sight for which I had been waiting all this while was right in front of me.

She was there. She lit the room up with her sheer presence.

Avantika.

She looked resplendent, radiant and beautiful. She was the girl of my dreams.

'I missed you,' she said.

I took her by her hand and closed the door behind her. She walked straight into the room and sat on the bed.

'I missed you too,' I said as I sat near her. She hugged me.

'Baby,' she said and I found both of us crying profusely in her embrace, which only got tighter with every passing second. I felt like an asshole. *Again.* I could not believe that I was dating such a sweet person. How could she forgive me! I felt so terribly guilty in her embrace. She loved me so much and yet I kept hurting her all time. I wished that I had a time machine so that I could go back in time and make everything all right for her. I do not know for how long we cried but we were in each other's embrace till the time the hostel corridor outside fell silent and we could hear the crickets in the room.

'Why did you go?' I asked her.

'I needed time.'

'Please don't do it again,' I kissed her.

'I will try not to.'

I wanted to ask her about Kabir, but I did not want to spoil it. But she asked, 'You're hanging out a lot with Malini?' she asked naughtily.

'Oh . . . you noticed?'

'Wasn't I supposed to?'

'Yes, you were. The only reason why I was with her was

because I wanted to catch your attention,' I said.

'You succeeded,' she said.

'All I want is you, Avantika. I am so sorry,' I said.

'Shhh . . .'

'I missed you so much.'

'I missed you too.'

'Have you forgiven me, Avantika?' I asked her. She did not say anything for a while.

'Deb . . .'

'Yes?'

'I love you. So much that it scares me,' she said.

'What do you mean?'

'I should have been angry at you that you kissed her. I was . . . but it only for a small while. I had forgiven you even before we reached college,' she said. The tears in her eyes had come back.

'You had? Then why did you need time?' I asked.

'I just got scared that I had forgiven you so easily. How could I love you so much? I mean . . . What if you leave me someday? What will happen to me then, Deb? What if you just decide to go?'

'I will never leave you . . .'

'That's what you said the last time . . . and you kissed her,' she said.

I had nothing to say. I felt ashamed. The power of her love for me always made me feel insignificant. She hugged me and I felt her sobbing silently. I was such a bad person. She deserved someone better.

We just talked that night. She broke down more than once. She told me how hard it was for her to get Malini out of her head. It was tougher for her than it was for me, she said. She told me that she had spent the last few weeks crying herself to sleep every day. Also, she told me that my countless messages gave her the strength to go through the days or it would have been a lot tougher for her. I was glad that I had not stopped texting her.

She said, *it is always tougher for a girl.*

'You didn't miss me as much as I did, did you?' I asked.

'I did.'

'Why Kabir wasn't as interesting?'

I do not know why on earth I was taking his name repeatedly. I was still jealous of the times Avantika had spent with him.

She turned my head and kissed me, 'No one can replace you baby,' she said. 'You are the best.' She went on to tell me that he was not as funny or as interesting as I was. My grin kept widening by every passing second.

'Thank you.'

'. . . and you owe me a treat Deb . . . a big one.'

'And why is that?'

'You ungrateful swine . . . I saved your ass from Verma! What else.'

'Yes, for that, you deserve one . . . should we call Kabir too?'

'Deb? Can you stop with the taunts?'

'Sure. Sorry.'

'. . . and I have better taunts in place. Malini and you . . . that's all I thought about in the past so many days,' she said.

I did not debate that. I had been unfair to her. A few days later, I came across a few poems she wrote in that period and every one of them was more painful than the previous one. Not a day has gone since, when I haven't regretted what I had done to her. She had been to hell and back, and it was definitely more painful than what I had been through, alone.

The next day, the eyeballs turned towards me for what used to be the original reason. *Avantika!* I could not complain one bit.

The next few days I followed Avantika like a shadow; never let her out of sight, and showered her with surprises every few hours. This is not an exaggeration. I wanted her to be so incredibly happy that she never thinks of leaving me again. Had I had more money, I would have changed her entire wardrobe in a matter of weeks. I was broke by the time she knocked sense in to my head and asked me to stop buying her things.

Those days, it was hard to wipe off that huge grin off my face. It was a feeling of constant elation to have her right by my side again. Just like the old times. Life was complete again, and I was falling in love all over again. For the millionth time, I guess, with the same girl every time.

'You really are wooing me all over again,' she said.

'You are a thing to be wooed over and over again baby.'

'Deb . . . You don't have to do it again. I am already yours,' she smiled lovingly.

'I wouldn't really mind doing it again . . .' I leaned onto her.

She slapped me away. 'Behave. This is a class!'

'So? You really have gotten old and boring!'

'And why do you say that . . .' she said.

'Remember? Last year?' I reminded her.

It was December, last year. She had challenged me that I could not get a CGPA in excess of 7. When I got a 7.08, it was payback time! We had made out in the Dean's office. I had jumped out of the window, just in time. We were so close to being screwed. Oh wait! We did get *screwed* . . . and it was awesome!

Mittal entered the class late and sat next to us.

'I told you she will be back,' Mittal said.

'Mittal, had it been up to you, you would have made him sleep with Malini,' Avantika butted in.

'But you still would have taken him back, right?'

'Why do you say that?' Avantika asked.

'Girls are *like* that! They might not forget . . . but they always forgive!' he said.

'I love him,' Avantika said and held my hand.

'Kiss me Avantika,' Mittal said, ' . . . and let's see if Deb forgives you and accepts you.'

'*Eww!*' Avantika remarked.

As soon as Mittal said this, there was an awkward silence. *What if Avantika does something? Would I?*

Avantika did not come up with something equally witty. I did not know what she was thinking, but the colour went off her face, and she looked away from us. Mittal's words bore heavy on us.

Every one stayed shut for a while before Mittal broke the silence, 'Anyway, since now you are off Malini . . .'

'I was never on her!' I butted.

'Whatever . . . but since you two are together again, I guess I have a chance at Malini again,' he said.

'I agree. Why can't you stick to one?' Avantika said.

'What's the use!' Mittal said. 'And frankly speaking, I have made so many girls cheat on their boyfriends that I can't trust anyone. I seriously do not want to subject myself to what Deb went through. The whole break up thing makes me sick . . . plus the sex is good, why fiddle with it . . .'

'Someday you will have to let go,' Avantika said.

Someone's phone beeped. It was Mittal's.

'Shit, mom!' he said. Immediately, he walked out of the class, frantically dealing some number.

'That wasn't his mom,' Avantika said.

'I don't think so,' I said.

It was some girl. *Who? Where? What?* There were no answers to these questions. Unless Mittal was actually a big momma's boy, which we all knew he wasn't. We had no idea whose female voice was on the other side.

Midterms were just two days away now, and it was just in time that Avantika and I had patched up again. The only good thing about a break-up is that the patch up sex is always great. So is the patch up love;. the patch up gifts; the patch up moments; the patch up tears. They all make up for the all lost time during the break-up. Whenever the time you were away from that person flashes in front of your eyes, it just makes you love the person even more. I did not want to lose her again, at any cost. If I had it my way, I would have just hugged her and *never* let her go.

'Will you stop staring and concentrate on the book?' Avantika said. 'And no, I don't mind you doing that, but you are distracting me.'

'I am sorry for that,' I said and looked down into my books. Her phone rang again, for the tenth time that day.

'Hey . . . my room . . . yes, he is here too . . . no, I will be here . . . how much have you done? . . . best of luck . . . c'mon, you will do it . . . you always do . . . yeah . . . yeah . . . haha . . . why not? . . . no . . . yeah . . . later . . . bye . . .'

She kept the phone down. I thought, I would not ask her, but I did, 'Kabir?'

'Yes.'

'And this is not distracting?'

'I didn't call him,' she said categorically, 'and gave the *shut-the-fuck-up* look. I did exactly that. I looked into my books and tried hard to concentrate, but all I could do was to relive the conversation again.

He is here too.

Did he want to come here?

I will be here.

He had offered her to come out?

No. Yeah, later . . . bye

She said no to what? What had he asked? I tried to frame as many questions as possible to it, each one made my head burst.

Say you love me? *No.*

But you do, right? *Yeah.*

Then, say it. *Later . . . bye.*

I wanted to grab her cell phone and check her dialled calls, received calls and inbox, but then I told myself that I was being paranoid. I looked at her staring deep into her books. She looked at me, smiled and got back to Brand Management. A few hours passed.

'How much have you done?' she asked and I told her the page number I was on.

'What the fuck are you doing?' she said and called me over. 'Is there something wrong?'

'No. I just love you,' I said.

'That is a nice thing to say and you can say it over and over again till your tongue's paralyzed, and then say it again, but that is no excuse for not studying,' she smiled and sat next to me.

She flipped through the pages and started to explain me each topic, took care that I listened to every word that she said and I understood everything. She probably used more time in explaining me everything than she had taken in studying everything herself.

'That is all I have done till now,' she said, tired from all the explaining.

'You are the best teacher, *ever.*'

'Only for you, baby,' she pulled my cheeks and kissed them.

'I am glad.'

'You want to stay here? Or go back to your room.'

It was two in the night, and I wasn't supposed to be in the girls' hostel.

'Is that even a valid question?'

'Not really,' she said and put her hands across me.

'I thought so.'

I kissed her. Tired after a lot of studying and some of extra-curricular activities, we lay next to each other. Her touch still got my nerves in a storm of emotions, predominantly lust, and I did not remember the last time we would have stopped at just a kiss. It was hard to stop myself from getting her out of her clothes.

'Isn't it so strange that even after three years, I can't keep my hands off you?' I said.

'Not really. I like to believe that I am incredibly good looking even after all these years,' she winked.

'Yeah . . . that is true too.'

'But a lot of other people are hot to you,' she taunted.

'It had nothing to do with *her* hotness.'

'It is okay baby,' she pecked me. 'I know. You still love me. So, it is kind of okay. But you do lust *her!*'

'I don't.'

'I don't care even if you do, not much. Love isn't lust, is it?' She said.

'No, it is not, not really . . . so, for you . . . what is love?' I said.

My mind went off to when Malini had asked me the question and I had replied that love for me was Avantika. A simple answer to a simple question! But Avantika was a girl, and females have a convoluted answer to every question, no matter how straightforward it is.

'Love . . . umm . . . is conversation.'

'Conversation? Are you trying to be intelligent?' I smirked.

'Firstly, I *am* intelligent, and second, no, it *is* just something that I feel.'

'Elaborate,' I said and hugged her tighter.

'Look Deb, right now . . . We are into all this . . . you know . . . trying to take each other down, getting our hands in all the strange tingly places all the time . . . but with time it will all go, you know . . . you will start using Viagra, my breasts will sag unless I spend millions on them! We will not be animals anymore . . . the sex part will not be that much fun . . .'

'I will pay for new boobs. Don't worry about that.'

'Shut up Deb . . . that's not the point. The point is . . . it will go. But we will still be together, and not for this. The only thing left then would be conversations. People's hips give away, they lose their teeth and they are still in love. And they are definitely not having sex. Or going to parties. They talk. The only thing that remains is *conversation*. That is all what will remain.'

'You have a point there.'

'So, what is lust?' I asked. I really had no interest in the conversation, I just really wanted to hug and sleep tight.

'Lust is lust! It's what we feel after the first kiss . . .' she smirked.

'And it has nothing to do with love?'

'Yeah . . . pretty much,' she said.

'But how do you get to the lust part if the love part, that is the first kiss part, doesn't happen?'

'Don't get in to technicalities now,' she said.

'Hmm . . .'

We slept in a while. Sometimes, I thought Avantika thought too much, but then it is a girl thing—*thinking*. They find it hard to accept that we, guys, are only after one thing—*sex*. Though, if sex comes with love, nothing better. For me, it did, and it was awesome!

'How did it go?' she asked, smiling, and I guessed she must have rocked it.

'It was okay.' I winked.

I had cheated. At the one-hour mark, Avantika and I had met at the water cooler and she had told me everything I could not answer in the paper. It was a ritual for us. It started with the first exam we gave at MDI. At first, we thought it was kinky to make out during exams, in washrooms. But later, we thought we could exchange notes and compare answers! And that's what we did in every exam. Slowly, it had become a habit. Yes, a few people had caught us on various occasions, but Avantika is too smart, and too good looking to be indicted in a cheating case.

'What plans tomorrow?' I asked. It was the last exam and as

it happens, one just stops giving a fuck, however, not Avantika.

'We decide tomorrow?' She said sternly.

'Okay.'

Kabir passed us as we walked to our own rooms to catch a little sleep. He smiled at Avantika and she smiled back. Kabir used to sit right in front of Avantika and they had quite a lot to chat just before the exam. Somehow.

'How did his exam go?' I asked her.

'What do you expect? He is Kabir.'

'And that is supposed to mean?'

'You know . . . he is like the ultimate geek . . .' she said. 'Now go sleep, Deb. See you in the evening,' she said. 'And no touching today. We screw up the last paper every time.'

'Cross my heart and hope to die.'

'We will see,' she winked.

'Hey.' I swung open the door as I moved into Avantika's room.

'Shhh . . .' she put a finger on my lips.

Avantika was on the phone and talked very formally to a heavy male voice on the other side of the phone. She talked about financials, return on investments, portfolios, the kind of stuff I knew nothing about. I sat in the corner waiting for the awesomely boring conversation to stop. Fifteen minutes passed and she was still yakking on the phone and now discussed about every mundane detail about MDI. I logged onto her Gmail chats and started reading her chats.

Chat with Deb. (250 lines)
Chat with Deb. (323 lines)
Chat with Deb. (298 lines)

Chat with Kabir. (150 lines)
Chat with Kabir. (50 lines)
Chat with Deb. (345 lines)

I clicked on her chats with Kabir. My heart pounded. They talked about nothing controversial. Their chats revolved around classes, careers and projects. *Harmless.* I sighed. There was nothing that offended me. Kabir had called her *'baby'* a few times, but he called every girl that. So . . . it was harmless. I felt a little bad as I checked her chats, as I had always found all this very intrusive. We never shared passwords, it just breeds more doubts.

'What are you doing?' she asked. I hadn't noticed that she had kept down the phone.

'Nothing.'

'Deb? Reading my chats? How rude!' she said and closed the window.

'Why? You have something to hide?'

'No. I do not. But if there would have been something to tell you, I would have told you by now. And if I have not, then probably I don't want you to know. Get it?' she said. She spoke so quickly, that all I could make out were her bright pink lips moving. And that in itself was not that bad a sight.

'In short does that mean you want to make out right now, right here?'

'Very funny,' she said. 'By the way, where is your book?'

'Book? What book? Easy one tomorrow. Just go through it once and tell me what's in there,' I said. Last exams are not meant to be studied for, everyone knows that, right?

'I am so not going to do that. You know I can't concentrate with you sitting there doing nothing there.'

'I will sit here and read something else that should work?'

'Maybe.'

'My baby. The sweetest! Oh . . . whose call was it?' I asked her.

'Kabir's father is floating a live project in MDI. And we are doing it.'

'What? Kabir? Our Kabir?'

'Oh . . . *our* Kabir?' she winked. 'Should I be jealous?'

'Tell me.'

'Yes. It is from him. He is getting it. I have given your name for it too. It would look good on our resumes'

'I am not interested,' I said.

'What? Don't be silly Deb, it isn't for me. I already have a placement. I don't need it. It will be good for you. And since I am in it, you don't even have to work for it.'

'I don't want to have to do anything with him.'

'But baby, I know you don't like him, but this is for your own good,' she said.

'I don't want it. Period.'

'Can we talk about it later?' she said.

'There is nothing to talk about it. If you want to do it, go ahead,' I said angrily.

'I just wanted it for you,' she said, as her mood dropped and shoulders slumped. She started marking her book, while I lay in the corner fuming. The whole Kabir thing was driving me crazy. I knew she was mine, but I could not help it. I sat there telling myself that she was mine, no wonder what comes her way. Thinking like that helped, a little. I did not study much that day. Avantika, just put things in my ear before we slept off. Thank God, it was a theory paper, or I would have been fucked badly.

And yes, we never did that live project. It was foolish of me.

As usual. Jealousy always got the better of me.

I was always the possessive, angry boyfriend.

'Sad crowd!' I shouted in her ear, her eyes glued to the big projector screen.

It was Liverpool Vs. Arsenal. She was an Arsenal fan, and it would be over her dead body that she would ever miss a match. I wasn't a big fan, neither of the game nor of the team. Her ex-boyfriend was an Arsenal fan and she had got this obsession from there. And I didn't quite like it.

'Shut up,' she said, as she stuffed her mouth with whatever came to our table. The score line was tied and from the little I knew of football, it was a tight match. I dared not to disturb her. I remember the last time I made fun of an Arsenal player, she didn't let me touch her for a week!

'Fu— ' she stopped herself from shouting aloud as the Liverpool goalie made a valiant save just before half time.

'Liverpool is going to suck them out in the next half.' A guy in a Liverpool t-shirt said out loud. It was aimed at Avantika. I put my hand over Avantika to calm her down. The last time someone had said something like that to her, she had thrown an ashtray at him. She had missed by an inch and we were thrown out of the place. This time she let the guy go with just a subtle expression of displeasure—the middle finger. He reciprocated with a more vulgar rendition the same. He was just trying to be a stud.

'I so want to knock the head off that guy,' she said.

'Calm down. Just a game!'

'Deb, this is the last time I am telling you . . . it is not JUST A GAME!'

'Yeah, yeah. It is a religion, right?'

'Yes,' she said.

'Hold this.' She gave me her handbag, 'I will just be back.'

She asked the waiter where the washroom was and headed towards it. The half time analysis ended, the match started again and the place was filled up with shouts of ecstasy and anguish. Avantika took more than usual; she hated to miss the first few minutes after the half time. I called her and her phone rang in her handbag. I took the phone out and started to fiddle with it. I often wondered how people used to get to know that their girlfriends/spouses were cheating on them before cell phones came along and made everyone's life hell.

Anyway, I have often heard people say, it takes just one thing to turn your life around and suck your heart out. I found *two*.

First. A photograph of her with Kabir's hand around her . . . when we were on a break.

Second. Muahhh! I wonder why I didn't find you earlier.

Ever felt like someone punched the guts out of you. The feeling was similar, if not worse. I felt puke-ish and had immediately gone red in the face. I got up from my chair, paced around my table and waited for her. I wished I had not looked into her cell phone. I tried hard to calm myself down. I sat down, opened that picture and kept it on the table. I picked up the cell phone more than once to see it while she was still in the washroom.

'You look . . . strange,' she said, as she walked up to me, smiling.

'What's this?' I said and pushed the phone in her hands.

'What?'

'The message! What is that? Care to *explain*, Avantika?'

'It's nothing . . .' she stuttered.

To see her stutter just deepened my suspicion. I was going berserk. It was not the picture, but the smile in it that hurt me more. She had every right to be happy, but somehow, I was enraged.

'When was this . . . tell me . . . Please tell me Avantika,' I said, barely keeping myself from shouting. The guy from the other table shouted *slut* to his friends. I looked at him and he looked away.

'I . . . Can we go?' she asked.

'Go? Where?'

'Can we just go back to college? Will explain you there?' she said.

I picked up my things and we left the place. I paced down to the car leaving her far behind. I fumed while I waited for her to come to the car. The car whizzed through the narrow lanes as I pushed the pedal as far as it could go. A few people escaped from being crushed beneath the wheel, jumping out of the way just in time.

'Calm down,' she said.

'Calm down? After seeing *this?* How the fuck can you let any guy talk to you like that? And Kabir? I was there killing myself after you left me and this is what you were up to.'

'Deb . . .'

'You were smiling and taking pictures and getting all mushy with him! You were storing it for posterity? Your sweetheart and you?' I said and pushed the pedal further down as we sped through the streets.

'Can we just talk about it?' She put her hand on my shoulder and I shrugged it off.

'We are TALKING about it!' I shouted and parked the car with a screech outside the hostel.

And I Lose My Mind

We were in her room again.

'TALK,' I shouted. I was just losing it.

'There is something I need to tell you,' she said.

'What?'

Now that she had something to tell, I really wished she had nothing to tell. I prayed and hoped there would be no story behind that picture and the offhand message. I was wrong. My life was about to change.

'*I kissed him,*' she said feebly.

My world fell apart. It broke into small tiny pieces beyond repair. I wished she had *lied*, not told me. The last few days had been good, why did she have to tell me? She did not! She could have just buried that deep inside and we could have gone on with our lives. Why the fuck did she have to come out with it?

'You *WHAT?*' I started shaking in my shoes, as it refused to sink in.

'I kissed him.'

I took a deep breath in.

'When? How? Why? Tell me *EVERYTHING. NOW,'* I had tears in my eyes as I shouted.

'We went out one day . . .'

'*TELL* me the *FUCKING* date, Avantika.'

'12th October.'

'Oh . . . so you remember the date too? So this is what you were goddamn doing when I was not there? Kissing other people. Who else did you kiss?'

'I was a little drunk.'

'Little drunk! We know you do not fucking get drunk Avantika.'

'I am sorry.'

'Sorry? What is it? You got bored with me? You were just looking for a break, weren't you? Malini just gave you that chance, didn't she?'

'It's—'

'You just kissed once?'

'Yes.'

'Was he a good kisser? Was he?' I said, and paced around the room. My head started to burst. I clenched my fist and wanted to hit something. Maybe, Kabir. I was freaking angry.

'Don't ask that.'

'*DON'T ASK THAT?* What does that mean? He was good, right? Why don't you fucking tell me? What else did you do?'

'Nothing.'

'Nothing? I don't believe you! You fucking slept with him, didn't you?' I accused her.

'I didn't,' she said.

'You fucking took two years to get over your previous guy and this is how long you take to get over me?'

'I wasn't trying to get over you,' she said and held her head.

'Then what the fuck was it? What the fuck was it? Swear on me you didn't do anything beyond the kiss?'

'Deb!'

'Just do it.'

'I swear.'

'Say the whole thing.'

'I swear nothing happened beyond the kiss, Deb. Don't make me do this.'

'Was he nice? Better than me?'

'Don't ask that.'

'Why? Why the fuck not! I can fucking ask you anything,' I shouted.

'I was drunk.'

'Swear on me you don't remember.'

'Don't make me swear,' she said.

'I will. I fucking will. So how was it? Huh? *HOW WAS IT?*'

'It was different,' she said.

'*Different?*'

'I don't know Deb. I was drunk and frustrated. It just happened.'

'You were getting back at me by kissing that son of a bitch?'

'I was not,' she said.

'Oh . . . you were! Don't bullshit me now. I am not a fool. You always liked him, didn't you? Why couldn't you just tell me!'

'But . . .'

'Got to hell, Avantika! Go! Sleep with him. I do not fucking care. I am ending this . . . right now, right here! I don't want to see your face ever again . . .'

'Deb?'

'I can't even see you right now Avantika. You disgust me!'

'I am sorry,' she said. She had tears in her eyes, but it did *not* matter. She had kissed someone else. I could not have accepted it. Of all the people, it was Kabir.

'Deb . . .'

'I hate you Avantika. Malini is so much better than you! Just go and sleep with Kabir . . . just go away!'

'But Deb . . .'

'I don't want you in my life. Go and sleep with him. Why did you come back Avantika? To hurt me?' I said and walked up to her and looked at her. She was crying. I didn't give a damn.

I continued, 'Mittal was right. I should look beyond you. You are a waste of time.'

I got up and slammed the door as I left. I felt like crying aloud and bang my head on the wall. Something that would make the hurt go away. What I said before leaving that room was unnecessary and I knew she would be crying for it. I wanted her to cry. She had been a slut and I did not give a fuck. It was *so* me. Those minutes in her room were the worst I had ever been through.

I had two options. Option one was get in to Kabir's room and get him beaten up. I liked that option. I wanted him to bleed. I wanted to break a few bones, maybe kick him in the nuts and do something that would keep him off Avantika. I wanted to *kill* him painfully. Take out his fingernails one by one, so that he screamed in pain. Something that would make him experience what I was going through.

Second, I could go in to Malini's room and sleep with her.

Avantika had been a slut. I could be too. I know I had kissed Malini but it was a mistake! She should have tried to make things better, not go and kiss another guy.

I picked a third option. I texted Avantika.

Drunk? You bloody took a picture of after it!

She replied.

Deb, I am really sorry, it meant nothing.

I messaged her back.

It was different right? He was better I am sure. Why don't you go to him? I won't be messaging you from now on. Bye baby. Take care.

She replied.

I am sorry. Nobody makes me feel the way you do. I did not even feel like kissing somebody. I don't even care how it was. It really meant nothing. It felt nothing.

It just made me angrier.

Bye Avantika.

A little later, I messaged her again.

Didn't you feel guilty?

She messaged back.

It killed me. It still is.

I replied.

That is why you still hung out with him even after it? Bullshit. Just go away Avantika. Isn't he seeing someone?

She replied.

No, he broke up a month back.

I messaged.1

So you were celebrating your break ups! Nice! Is that why you kissed him? You were waiting for him to break up or what?

She replied.

It's nothing like that Deb.

I messaged.

I know nothing about you. You didn't miss me. You were kissing him. Please don't message me after this. I won't. bye.

I threw my phone on the bed and held my bursting head. I thought of talking about it to Malini, Shashank . . . or Mittal. It felt so wrong telling them. I do not know what stopped me. Avantika had kissed someone else. I did not want people to think of her as a slut.

I just could not shake off the image. Kabir and Avantika kissing. I talked to myself the whole night, trying to think like her, think like me and do something to soothe myself. No matter how hard I tried, I could not stop. I kept talking to myself!

She was just alone. And frustrated. There have been times when you have wanted to kiss Malini again, haven't you? No, I have not, they were just passing thoughts. No they weren't, that was just because you wanted to feel a little different, a little better. So what if she did? But she kissed him. I didn't kiss Malini. But you wanted to. But I didn't, that is the point. She did and she didn't even feel guilty about it, she was still talking to her after it. How can she do that? Didn't she feel guilty? Didn't she think what it could do to our relationship?

How can she lie so blatantly? I fucking told her the moment I came from Mumbai about what happened. How can she not tell me? So many days passed? How can she not? I was not even in my senses when that fucking happened. She is such a . . . .no she is not . . . She did everything for me. Things that I wouldn't do for her. But why this? Was she getting bored? She had always been on the lusty side? But she always said I made her so. She once said, lust and love is different . . . but she fucking kissed him . . . she kissed him . . . and then took a picture. What? Preserving memories . . . she didn't even think that every time she sees it, it will come back to her? She wouldn't feel guilty then? What if she is still lying?

I can't see him. I can't see her. How can I possibly see her walking around with him? Or how can I just see Kabir? That bastard of a guy. Walking around . . . . . . he just kissed her . . . The most beautiful girl in the college . . . He kissed my girlfriend . . . wouldn't he be so proud of doing what he did, making a girl like Avantika kiss him . . . can I just make Mittal send some guys after him. Should I? But is it his fault? Not really. Who wouldn't kiss her? Who wouldn't want to kiss her? Fuck man . . . what the fuck should I do. I want her. I so want her right now. I wish she would just hug her and tell me that everything will be fine. And tell me that I was better. The kiss. Tell me that she missed me.

I did not know what to do. This thing was totally screwing up my head. I could not sleep. The images kept flashing through my head; every minute; every second.

I did not sleep for a single second that night. The only reason I did not want to go to class the next day was because I would have to see his ugly bastard face the next day. I could not take it anymore.

I had to forgive her. She had forgiven me too. There was no excusable reason for me to do what I was doing for her. I was just being revengeful, sadistic and foolish. I still loved her, and she still loved me. I had to go back to her. I just had to. I could not have let Kabir come between us.

I called her up.

And Again

'Hi,' I called her up.

'Hi Deb.'

'What are you doing?' she asked.

'Nothing, was reading the newspaper . . . and . . . I don't remember the last time I read it.' We had been going out for three years and this was probably the first time that we having such small talk.

'I know about that, Deb,' she said.

'Look Avantika . . . despite what you told me, despite what happened, I have missed you. The past few hours have been the most traumatic of my life. I have never felt more suicidal. I just want you back. I miss you . . .'

'I missed you too . . . and I am sorry about what happened. I really am,' she said, still crying.

'I know, Avantika. It's just that it's hard not to think about it.'

'I know, Deb . . .'

'I am sorry for acting so immaturely Avantika. I should have understood. I mean even I kissed Malini and you understood. I am sorry for being such an ass.'

'Is that why you forgive me? Because I forgave you for kissing

Malini?' she asked.

'No! I just understand I love you too much to leave you like that. It would be foolish and unfair.'

'I am sorry, Deb.'

'It's okay, Avantika.' I said. I heard her sniffing from the other side of the phone. She was still crying profusely.

'What's the matter?'

'I don't deserve you, Deb' she said.

'You? Are you crazy? You are a saint. I mean, almost . . . You are too good for me,' I assured her. Had she been in front of me, I would have hugged her and made things all right.

'You don't understand, Deb.'

'What do I not understand?'

'You told me everything. You believed in me. You let me know everything and never did anything from me.'

'So . . . so . . . what do you mean?' I said, a little puzzled, a little scared.

'Nothing.'

'*TELL ME.* Did you hide *something?*'

'I lied . . .'

'What? What did you lie about?' I asked. The pain came rushing back.

'I don't want to hurt you anymore,' she said. 'You should just leave me.'

'What? *TELL* me clearly, Avantika. Please don't play games with me,' I said.

'. . . Kabir and I . . . we went beyond . . .' she stopped.

My heart stopped. I was numb. My mind went into multiple convulsions. '*Wh . . . what? What?*'

'Just leave me, Deb. I am not worth it. I wish I could just die.'

'I want to know. Just tell me what you did with him.'

'Please Deb, just leave me. I am fine. I am sorry. We should not be together . . .'

'It is not about you. It is about me! I want to know. Tell me.'

'I don't want you to know.' She was still crying. 'I don't want to hurt your more than I already have . . .'

'*I WANT TO KNOW,*' I shouted.

'Something more happened . . .'

'Wh . . . what? What happened . . . What else . . . what else happened?' I stuttered and stammered. My eyes welled up.

'Deb . . .'

'You made out? He fucked you? What did you do? Just tell me. When did it happen? Where did you do it?'

'We went to his place,' she said.

'You went to his place that day? I saw you in college. I fucking saw you in college. And you swore on me . . . but you swore on me.'

'I lied,' she said.

'Tell me what happened . . . when . . . please do *not* fuck around. I want the truth, right now,' I said.

'It was some other day,' she said.

'You kissed him twice? You made out?' I had tears in my eyes.

'Yes,' she said.

'You're such a slut, Avantika! You're still sleeping with him, aren't you?' *Fuck! This cannot be happening. This cannot be true.* The tears had started to flow down now. My heart was being crushed every second.

'No, I'm not!'

'He fucked you? Didn't he?'

'No,' she said.

I was losing my mind. My girlfriend was nothing but a slut. Just a few weeks, and she could not keep her hands off another guy. *Why!* Was I not good enough?

'Why did you do it, Avantika? *Why?*'

I sat in the corner of the room. I was no longer angry. I just felt defeated. My love had no meaning for her. She had disrespected my love of so many years. I cried and held my head in my hands. I did not know what to say to her. This was over. She had slept with him, twice. She was not drunk and it was not a mistake. My mind went into tingles. Just the thought that someone else touched her made me go crazy. She was *mine*. How could she do it! How can she? I cried and cried and hoped I would find an answer. I loved her so much. Why did she do it to me? What wrong had I done? Such a big revenge for I kissed Malini? I was fucking drunk! Did I deserve that punishment?

'I think this is the last time we are talking Avantika. Thank you so much for sleeping around. I never thought you would . . .' I found it so hard not to cry.

'I am sorry, Deb. Please don't cry.'

'You don't have to be. Why didn't you just tell me that you wanted someone better? I would have moved out of your life! Why? Avantika?'

'Please don't cry, Deb. I didn't mean for anything of this sort to happen.'

'Do you love him? Kabir?' I asked. I was still crying my heart out. I did not know what else to do. My life had ended. I could have just slit my wrist and put an end to all the pain. I could have made those images of a naked Avantika with Kabir go away. All I needed was a knife.

'I don't love him,' she said, 'I love you.'

'Oh, so you love me and still you sleep with him? What are

you Avantika? Did he fucking pay you?'

'Deb!'

'Fuck you, Avantika. Why didn't you just tell me! Why make me go through all this!' I cried out lied. I punched my fist on the wall. It pained but it was nowhere near to what Avantika made me feel. I already felt dead.

'Yes, I shouldn't. Even if you say something, how do I believe you? How the fuck am I supposed to believe? You swore Avantika . . .'

'Deb, I will always love you. I always have,' she said.

'He was better than me, wasn't he?'

'Why are you asking me that? Does that matter?' She was still crying as she said that. I did not care about her tears; I cared about mine.

'It does matter. Of course, it matters. It matters. You sleep with him. Not once, but twice and you say it shouldn't matter? I want to know why you did it!'

'I am sorry, Deb.'

'Why did you come back to me? Why? He is single, he is good in bed, why don't you go back to him? Why don't you? Just go . . .'

'There is nothing. Please stop crying, Deb.'

'How many guys have you slept with in the last three years? Two? Three?'

'No, Deb, what are you talking . . .' she said, she was wailing now.

'How do I believe you?'

'Why would I lie now?'

'I don't believe a single thing you say Avantika. You are just . . . You love him, right?'

'Please don't say that Deb. He does nothing to me . . . I was just . . .' She was barely audible behind all the crying. I wanted her to cry more. More than I cried. I wanted her to just go away.

'You are such a . . .'

'Slut? Say it,' she said.

'I won't. Just go. Bye Avantika. Just tell me before you go.'

'What?' she cried.

'Was he better than me?'

'I am not comparing an awful mistake with what I have loved the most.'

'Then this is the last time we are talking. *Ever.* Have a great time with him. Go. Sleep with him. I do *not* give a damn. Our relationship was the biggest mistake. I should have never . . .'

'Listen, Deb. It was nothing. It meant nothing. You know that. I do not care what happened. Just listen to me. Nobody can make me feel like you do. I lost it to you. That is what matters. That is all that matters,' she cried aloud. 'It was nothing. I do not want to compare anything that I had with you anyone else. I cannot. I don't care about anything else.'

'I do. I fucking do. You are not mine anymore. You are no longer my Avantika. Just go.'

I clicked the phone down and threw the cell phone across the room. The phone hit the wall and it broke into many pieces. The phone was dead. And with that a part of me died within.

The tears stopped to flow. It felt like someone had ripped apart my heart. I lost the will to live. My head burst and I wanted to bang it against the wall. I wanted to kill myself. How could I not see that before? Avantika always deserved someone better than me.

She had finally given into the temptation. In those moments, if I had a gun, I would have used it. I would have killed myself and relieved myself of the pain.

A Part of me Died

She was sitting there on the first seat. *Alone.* I took my seat in the third row. It seemed she had not slept the last night. I felt no love, only anger and disgust. And immense pain. It was excruciating just to see her. All those images of Kabir and her . . . I wanted to die. I so wanted to die. I was not strong enough to bear this pain. I had given the relationship three years, and she was everything I wanted from life. Now that she was no longer mine, life had lost all meaning.

'Another fight?' Shashank asked.

'I broke up.'

'What? What did you do?'

'I broke up and I don't want to talk to about it.'

'So does that mean you are going to start talking to Malini again?' Mittal asked.

'I don't know.'

'Then know it! She finally picked up my call yesterday. She even broke up with her boyfriend; a vulnerable moment for her, I don't want to miss it,' Mittal chuckled.

'I don't know whether I am going to talk to her or not, but

you stay away from her. She is a nice girl and she doesn't deserve you treating her like that. Just leave her alone if you can't be with her.'

'Relationship advice from you? You just left your girlfriend,' he said and it was unpleasant.

'Will you two calm down? Mittal, stay away from Malini, and Deb, sort out your thing with Avantika.'

Shashank said, and just as he asked us to stay quiet, the professor saw the three of us talking and asked us to shut up.

I looked at Kabir. He sat just behind Avantika and tried to initiate a conversation once or twice with her. I saw no reaction from her side. Nevertheless, I felt disgusted at the mere sight of him. Every few minutes, my head spun around the same topic.

Why? How? What made her?

I kept looking for these answers. The classes were a pain. I just waited for the ordeal to end, for her to get out of my sight. But how was I supposed to get her out of my mind? How was I supposed to shut my mind and not think about these two? *How?* I thought and struggled, until my head burst.

I sat there and weighed my options. Dying seemed very lucrative; jumping off the building was a great option. I looked for answers to soothe myself and take my mind off her. Nothing seemed to work. Every second, I felt as if I was being torn apart. The pain was too much for me to take. I needed alcohol, and I needed it fast. Then, I found my answer, *the girl with tiny bottles of vodka beneath her bed.*

Yes! That was the answer to my troubles. I needed a drink and I needed a friend. Soon, I was on my way to Malini's room. Revenge is sweet, I thought. That was the only way I could have made the pain go away. I wanted to help myself. I wanted to feel not killing myself.

I sprayed myself with a shitload of deodorant and rushed to her room. I looked around and saw no one watching. I ran through the corridor, reached her room and locked the room behind me.

'You want to talk about it?' Malini said.

I told her whatever had happened, detailing everything that happened. It surprised me as to how clearly I recalled every moment of it. It was etched in my memory. I remembered every single detail of it.

'Is that reason enough to leave her?'

I was not listening to her now. I had spent a month without her before. I could live another one. And maybe another one. I could do without her, I foolishly told myself.

'I just can't get her images out of my head.'

'What about her images?'

'Her images?'

'Of you and me kissing. Must be troublesome for her, right?'

'Yes, it would be. But I was drunk, crazy drunk and secondly, I didn't hide it from her. She did. She fucking did. I was wrong. But she is more wrong. She fucking made out with him!'

'There is nothing like more wrong. What's wrong is wrong. And she took you back.'

'Yes, but after a month. She was sleeping with him all that time!' I said, still pissed off.

'And we know what it did to you. You were crushed Deb . . . Why subject her to the same? Do you even know what she must be going at that time? Have you tried thinking about that? Revenge is not the way to go.'

'It is not revenge. You wouldn't know about what I am going through.'

'I wouldn't?' she asked and raised her eyebrows.

As soon as I said it, I realized that Mittal had told me about her break up with her boyfriend. I tried to say that I was sorry for her, but she said, I did not need to care and asked me skip the topic.

My head was still hurting. My heart was bursting. I felt sick in the stomach thinking of those two. I was going crazy and she was not helping. I wanted someone to say that I was right, she was wrong, and Malini was not even coming close.

'So?'

'Do you have something to drink?' I asked her.

'Why?'

'Do you?' I asked sternly.

'Yes.'

She fished out a whiskey and a vodka bottle from beneath her bed. I grabbed the bottle and unscrewed it.

'You are not drinking from it,' she said. By the time she had said it, I had already taken a ten-second gulp on it. It burned my throat and everything else it touched. My head felt a little better.

'Here, all yours,' I said and passed on the bottle. I don't know what I was doing then. I was angry as hell. Maybe I wanted to get her drunk, make out and get back at Avantika as soon as possible. *I fucked Malini and she was better than you*, I wish I could tell Avantika and make her feel my pain. I do not know what I wanted. I just wanted to get it out of my head.

'I don't want to drink,' Malini said.

'Please?'

'Come. Sit here, 'she pulled my hand and made me sit on

the floor on the mats at the corner of the room.

'What happened?' I took another huge glug, my head spinning a little. But it was still hurting from everything that happened. Every single lie hurt. Every single thing she had said kept going on in my heard. How was I to believe she was not lying now?

Kabir could be up there in her room right now. They could be laughing at me! Maybe Avantika just wanted me out of her life. Though Avantika's messages kept pouring in. She said how sorry she was and how much she loved me, but it was hard to believe anything that she said right now.

'They made out,' I said and tears streaked down. I was getting disoriented and drunk.

'But Deb, you forgave her for kissing Kabir, didn't you?'

'She told me she had just kissed. She lied to me! Who knows what all she did?'

'Hmm . . . But didn't she take you back after you cheated on her?'

'I don't want to talk about it. Moreover, I just kissed you. I didn't make out,' I defended myself.

'Fine.'

She said and dangled the bottle in front of me. 'This will help?'

'Yes,' I said and took another huge glug. I didn't know how much I consumed, but I started to feel a little numb.

'Why are you here?' she asked.

'I like you Malini.'

'No, you don't,' she said.

'Yes, I do. Mittal says you are sexy. I think so too.'

'You are drunk.'

'I am?' I chuckled. 'I think we should make out! Yes, we

should! And then I will tell her that I slept with you. That would be great, isn't it?'

'Deb. Get a hold.'

'Nobody loves me!'

Her tone was stern and I could get it even despite my drunken state. She asked me to get up and pulled me up.

'Where are we going?'

'Nowhere. You are going to bed,' she said and helped me up. She tried to steady my wayward steps.

'Are we making out?' I smiled stupidly at her.

'No, we are not. Just sleep here.'

'I don't want to sleep yet.'

'You need rest,' she said as I climbed up the bed.

'I need you . . . and I am not drunk. Have you ever explored the possibility of us together? You are hot and I am ugly! Opposites attract, Malini!'

'You should sleep.'

'I am not sleepy.'

'No, I have not considered the possibility,' she said.

'Why haven't you?'

'You are not my thing,' she said.

'You haven't seen my thing.' I smiled.

'Not interested,' she said.

'Someday.'

I took another huge glug. Black. Blank. Darkness.

Of Life Without Her

I pulled the blanket over me. My head was hurting, and I felt terrible. The bed did not feel familiar. The room did not feel the same. I wasn't in Avantika's room. I woke up, my head hurt, and my lips were dry from the alcohol I had last night. *Malini's room.*

Everything came rushing back. *Fuck. She slept with him.*

Malini was not around. Bits of pieces from whatever I had said last night came back to me. I felt stupid. I looked at the time. 12:30pm. Straight ahead, I saw a note sticking from the mirror.

> *Good Morning. Water—Table. Breakfast—Table, leave it if it gets cold.*
>
> *Leave the room unlocked when you leave. Don't make it look like you stayed over.*
>
> *Take care. I will ask Mittal for your proxy.*
>
> *P.S. You drink like a little girl.*

The last line got a smile to my face. I drank the water and had a bite. The food had gotten cold but it felt good. I hadn't eaten well since the last few days. I washed up a little and left her room. On my way back, the same thoughts clouded my mind—Kabir and Avantika. I checked my cell phone. There were twenty messages; all of them were from Avantika.

I read them one after the other. They all said the same things.

> *I am sorry, Deb. You mean everything to me. You can leave me if you want to, but . . . I love you and I will always be yours. Our relationship meant everything to me. It was the only beautiful thing in my life. Try not to hate me. I love you and I will always do. I am sorry for what happened and I regret it more than anything in my life. I love you so much, Deb. Your leaving me is the worst thing that ever happened to me. You were my only family.*

I cried after I read all her messages. But she slept with someone else. A few messages would not change that. I could not trust her anymore. I felt so repulsed, hurt and humiliated in whole situation. The sickness returned to the stomach.

There was not a moment in that entire day that I was not thinking about it. I attended no classes that day. I waited outside the class of the last lecture and saw Avantika leave the class alone. Kabir left it with his guys. Avantika's eyes and mine met briefly. The tears were evident.

I walked right past her and hugged Malini.

'Going somewhere?' she asked.

'To see you and thank you!' I said.

'For?'

'The breakfast, the note . . .'

'Never mind,' she said. 'How are you today?'

'Better. Slightly. I am sorry for being so stupid last night. I was having a hard time . . .'

'I understand.'

'Coffee?' I asked her.

She did not say anything and we headed to the canteen. I saw Mittal and Shashank cross us; they looked at me with questions in their eyes. I met their eyes with no answers in mine. I had none.

'So?' she asked as she sipped on the coffee.

'How was the class?' I sighed.

'The usual. And we are supposed to talk about classes?' she said sarcastically.

'As in?'

'Why are you running away?'

'Running away? I am not running away.'

'Yes. You are,' she said. 'You were going back to her when she said she just kissed. But now that she took a few clothes off and made out, you can't take her back? What kind of a guy are you?'

'Listen to me. It was different. I was *not* in my senses. She *was* and she kissed him twice.'

'You kissed me twice, Deb.'

'I was sloshed the first time. And I didn't lie about it,' I said.

'She didn't want to hurt you.'

'Hurt me? Didn't she think about that when she kissed and made out with him?'

'Deb, you are such a loser.'

'Why?'

'Imagine. She made out just once. Not *twice* just *once*. Would you have taken her back?'

'Umm . . . yes . . . totally.'

I said it, but I was not so sure. I felt shallow. Why did I have a problem? Was it because Avantika had made out *twice?* Or was it because she had gone a step further than I had. I had kissed Malini, but she had made out. Was *that* the root of my problem? I felt cheap and unfair, but I could not do anything about it. I was hurt and I was not ready to accept her.

'You're just a jealous, chauvinistic man,' Malini said.

Maybe I was. Avantika should not have made out with him. Period.

'Now what?' Shashank asked.

'Nothing. I am just taking a break.'

'What the hell are you doing? Placements are in a week and you are doing such stunts in your life. Don't fuck them up man.'

He gave me a list of companies he had applied on my behalf and what all forms I had to fill up. He mailed me a file that had everything that I had to brush up before the placement week. He was a lifesaver when it came to such things.

But more than that, he kept on reminding me of my foolishness and how stupidly I was acting. He kept saying things like Avantika and I were supposed to be together! These things had always brought joy to me earlier, but now it just hurt me and reminded me of what had happened.

I crossed Mittal who was as usual on the phone. It was shocking because I was yet to hear him talk so meekly to someone. It was a girl for sure. But I was too occupied to care. I grabbed a few books from my room to prepare for the placement week. Shashank, Avantika and even Mittal, they all had offers and didn't need to study, I had to. I concentrated hard enough to kick her out of my mind for a few moments, hard enough, to bring tears to my eyes.

The evening was still a little productive, after Malini joined me in the library and marked out the exact things that would be useful. Over the next week or so, Malini took up Avantika's role. She made herself responsible for everything I did. She made sure I studied, and I know she did well because even Shashank was impressed with the kind of preparation I had before the placement week.

Two weeks had passed since that day, and the hurt was still there. But the days became a little more bearable. What really helped was that I got placed within the first few hours of the placement week. In a reputed FMCG with a package that made people more uncomfortable, than be happy about me. I spent entire days with Malini, so that kept my mind off Avantika.

Every day Avantika sent me messages, mails, and many missed calls to tell me how much she still loved and cared for me. Avantika told me how hard it was for her to live without me and that she would understand if I leave her.

She sent me all the mails and chats we had exchanged over the past three years. She reminded me everything that had happened, everything that we had seen together, every happy moment that we had spent smiling and every sad moment we had spent in each other hands.

'Are we never going to talk?' Avantika had called me up.

'No, Avantika,' I said.

'Can't we sort it out?' she said. I could sense that she was crying.

'No, we can't,' I said and cut the phone. She cried. She mailed. She wept. I was still being the angry asshole. I replied when I wanted to and rejected every call of hers. Somehow, it gave me a sadistic pleasure to see her go through what she had made me a few weeks earlier. I was yet to see her with Kabir in college.

I used to feel bad about her but I could not forgive her. It was too hard. Shashank and Mittal had asked a million times as to what had happened between the two of us, but I could not make myself to tell them.

Male ego, Malini used to tell me.

'You will be a lesser man,' she said.

'What?'

'Your girlfriend goes out and makes out with someone else. Where does that leave you? It just says that you're not good enough.'

'That's nonsense.'

That was not true. The only reason why I didn't tell anyone was because I didn't want people to look at Avantika like she was slut. Despite what happened, she would always be my little baby. I knew I would never stop loving her. But I knew I had to stay away from her.

'Can we stop talking about her?' I said irritably.

'I talk about her?'

'Whatever. But don't encourage my conversations from now on.'

'As you say.'

I used to crib a lot about my break-up. I could only discuss it with Malini as she was the only one who knew everything. A few minutes of silence passed.

'See, we have nothing else to talk about,' she said and smiled. 'The only reason we talk is because you love Avantika and you need her in your life.'

'Whatever,' I said.

⌒

It was barely a month left for college. We barely had any classes those days. A few classes dispersed through the week. The professors no longer cared about attendance or quizzes and made our lives a lot easier.

Slowly and steadily, Avantika's messages took a different tone. The number of messages increased but they were no longer *sorry* messages. They were just messages that said how much she missed me and what my love meant for her, about how much she would treasure me and all that bullshit.

She said she would always wait for me and that there would be no one who would ever be as important as I was for her. I couldn't say these messages didn't affect me. They killed me and often made me cry. It was not a break anymore. It was a break-up. And it hurt as much as I had heard it does.

Sometimes, when the nights fell, I used to give in. But the mornings used to get back all the bitterness with it and I used to hate her all over again. There were times that I desperately wanted to talk to her, but the presence of Kabir around the campus killed every bit of this urge.

She had done wrong, and she deserved it. Everyone around me would have agreed. Or not. I do not care.

Late one night, I called her up. As soon as I heard her voice, my heart melted and spilled on to the floor. I nevertheless tried to be stern.

'How are you?' I asked her.

'I am fine. How are you doing?'

'I am doing okay,' I said. *I am dying without you Avantika.*

'How did the exams go?'

'They went okay,' I said. Malini had taught me this time.

'Hmm . . .'

'Avantika?'

'Yes?'

'Just tell me something?'

'Say?' she said.

'Did you not think of me while you were doing it?' I tried to sound very soft. My temper was through the roof.

'I told you that I missed you while I was with him. I am sorry.'

'Is *sorry* going to work Avantika? After all that we had seen together? This is what you give me? This?' I tried to be as soft as possible.

'Why is it so important Deb? Can't we see through this?'

'See through this? What are you talking about? How am I supposed to let this go? I go and sleep with Malini every day from now on and come back to you, would you have me back? Would *you*?'

'I would. It wouldn't make a difference to me, Deb. I love you and I always will. You can go sleep with anybody you want to. But if you love me, I would still take you back. That's how much I love you.'

'Is that why you broke up for a month when I kissed Malini?'

'Trust me.'

'You disgust me. Avantika. You disgust me. You were such a mistake . . .'

I cut the phone. I do not know why I said such things. Maybe, I just wanted to hurt her and make her go through the pain that I was going through. Sometimes, the pain is so constant and deep that you learn to live with it.

At times like this, you are reminded of the pain and you

just can't deal with it. And more often than not, you end up saying things to the other that you don't even mean.

Do I disgust you? she messaged.

The time lag had lessened my anger and my propensity to hurt her.

Not really. I replied.

At certain levels, she did disgust me. I was disgusted at the fact that she was with him. I was disgusted that she lied to me. I was disgusted that I had to find out everything that she did by myself.

Of Life with Malini

'How long do you plan to stay away from her?' Malini asked.

'Fifteen more days and college would end. She would go her own way and I will have a new life. I will get over her. So, I plan to stay away from her forever.'

'Why do you want to get over her when you know you could be much better with her?'

'I am good. I am doing well.'

'I wasn't talking about your exams,' she smirked.

Quite surprisingly, I had done well in the last exams of the college. The credit went to Malini this time. She taught me this time. I had not touched a book myself. I couldn't. Avantika had not done too great. She had done terrible in fact.

Fifteen more days! It just struck me! College was about to get over.

There were just fifteen days left for the classes to end, for the convocation and the farewell party. Just a few formalities were all that was left of our college life. It sucked. Two years . . . gone, just like that. Time had simply whizzed by! The first one and half had been awesome to say the least. The last part of it pretty much sucked.

My joining date had come. I would have a few months before I would join the company. That meant I would have nothing to do for that time. It scared me. *What would I do!* Those three months of no college, and no job, would be tough as hell, I knew that. I missed Avantika.

Avantika and I had already decided how we would stay together, once again, if our jobs would have taken us to the same city. But these were the least important of our plans. I was already twenty-five. I had started to feel a little older than usual. We had never explicitly talked about it, but we knew it was on our minds. We had talked about it in undertones. We had to plan long term—better sooner than later.

'Why don't you call her?' she said when she saw me making circles with dirt on the canteen table.

'It's not helping. I called Avantika five times in five days, and it is all the same. I can't get it out of my head, I never will. We can never be together again.'

'Why not!'

'I can't forget what happened,' I said.

'What does she say?'

'. . . that she loves me, that whatever she did was a mistake, and it shouldn't matter if I love her.'

'Isn't she right?'

'No. The bitterness will stay. It will always stay. I will never forget what happened and I will never love her the same. I wouldn't ever be able to trust her again. She lied to me. I can never forgive her. It's better for her that we don't get together.'

'For her? All you are thinking about yourself. You and your

male ego is all that matters to you . . .'

'I don't know what it is but I just can't be with her. Not right now.'

'Don't make it too late,' Malini said.

'I don't care.'

'You do care. Have you seen yourself? You are a shadow of the guy you once were. Where is that smile that used to be on your face? Where is that cute God darn dimple? You don't jump around and do the stupid things you used to. You have changed.'

'Hmm.'

'Just stop being such a jerk. Look at her? Don't you feel sorry for her? She is alone and she cries all day. Why are you doing this to her? She loves you,' she said.

'Why are you taking her side?'

'I am not taking her side.'

'She slept around, not me! Avantika will be fine. She will go to Mumbai with Kabir and they will be fine,' I said. Just thinking about it killed me from inside.

'You know . . .'

'Malini? Can we stop talking about it?' I shouted.

'Fine,' she said.

She shut up. I had pissed her off. We didn't speak a word for the next hour. Malini used to put up with my irrational mood swings those days. She was being unrealistically sweet to me.

'I am sorry, Malini,' I said.

'For what?'

'For shouting at you . . . usually, messing up your life, I didn't want you to get involved in this.'

'If you hadn't noticed I wasn't doing anything constructive

before you came along and I ruined your life,' she said, with guilt in her voice.

'You didn't do that.'

'I did. If it were not for me, you would still be with her. Both of you would have been smiling . . . and look at you. I totally ruined your relationship.'

'. . . that you did,' I joked and smiled at her, '. . . though I like you!'

'You don't have to fall in love with me,' she smirked playfully.

'I need a rebound. I deserve one,' I said.

'Stop flirting!' She smiled. *Did I see a blush there?*

'Why?'

'Because you are making me feel good,' she said.

'And that is when I haven't even kissed you.'

'The last time you kissed me wasn't the most pleasant of experiences.'

She winked.

For the first time in weeks, we talked about something other than my break-up and Avantika. She recounted about her time in Canada. For the first time, she was being utterly chirpy and bubbly and I liked the new side of hers. Guys destroy everything. We are the ones responsible for wiping those smiles right off their faces!

It was one of those nights that Avantika and I had always looked forward to, I had imagined how would it be a million times.

The farewell night.

We had seen the senior farewell night. There was unlimited booze, ear blasting music and everybody dressed up his or her best! Everyone got sloshed. The outgoing batch danced like crazy. There were last minute proposals and rejections. There were many casual make-outs too! It was supposed to be a crazy night!

We had lived it before it happened. I had only imagined how good Avantika would look that day. She would have looked stunning. I remember she said once that she would wear a light pink *saree* that day. I had even gone on to imagining myself unwrapping her out of that *saree*!

Things change.

She was not there that night. I looked everywhere but I could not find her. I spotted every friend of hers. Even Kabir was there but she was nowhere to be seen. It seemed like it was not meant to be. I missed her so much that day. I just wished things to go back to what they were before.

Shashank and Mittal were with their girls and asked me where Avantika was. I had no idea. I started to ask around. After about half an hour, a classmate of ours said that she had talked to Avantika that morning. She was leaving for her local guardians place.

Local guardian?

She had no local guardian. The only local guardian where she could go to was in Mumbai . . . she could not have left? Or had she? Panic set in.

How can she leave? She did not even wish goodbye! Was I that unimportant? Is she already over me?

I ran to her hostel. It was locked. It was not her lock; it was a lock with an MDI emblem embossed on it. She had given up the room and she was not coming back. If only had I known that the night we fought would be the last night there, I would have done something. My fingers trembled. *Where is she?* I called her up but her phone was out of reach.

Flight? Already?

I could not get over the fact that the last time I would see her in the college was gone. The last time I had seen her in that room had passed. We would never be in that room together . . . *never* again. The urge to talk to her got tears to my eyes. I called her again. It was still switched off.

I was totally going nuts. I didn't know what to do. I started typing a message. I had to write '*call me.*' I ended up with a lot more. I sat on those stairs with tears in my eyes and Avantika on my mind . . .

If I'd only known . . .
That this is the last time we've met,
I would have stopped the break of dawn.
And stopped the sun to set . . .

If I'd only known
That I wouldn't ever see you again,
I would have framed a picture of you within,
To end my suffering, to end my pain.

If I'd only known,
That this is d last time I sit by your side,
I would have told u how much I loved you,
Keeping rest things aside.

If I'd only known,
That we would never hold hands again,
I would have held them strong,
N never let anything go wrong.

If I'd only known,
That you would stand always by my side,
I would have fought d world for you,
Breaking all d walls through,

If I'd only known,
That your love was true,
If I'd only known that you would come back soon,
I would have waited for you to come by,

If I'd only known any of this,
That you were what I was breathing for,
I would have breathed my last for you,
Seen you enough and bid you adieu,
While all I can do now,
Is sit here . . .
. . . and wait.
Love you.

If I'd only known . . .

I fiddled with the send button for quite some time as I sat there alone. Images from the numerous nights we had spent together in that room flashed in my mind. I lost it. I had tears in my eyes as I read my message. I wish I had done something about it. It sucked to let her go.

'There you are,' Malini said as she found me. I saved the message in the drafts.

'You were looking for me?' I collected myself.

'All over the place,' she said. She was genuinely concerned.

I reached out for the drafts. DELETE. I hit the button. It asked, *Are you sure you want to delete this?*

No.

'Let's go,' I said.

I tried not to look at her. We headed towards my car and left the campus. I just looked at her once for her approval and she seemed to be telling me that she was okay with wherever I wanted to go.

'Missing her?'

'You must just hate me?' I asked Malini.

She was probably the best dressed on the farewell that day, since her only competition had decided not to turn up. Her backless blouse showed every bit of her spotless white back and the tiny straps threatened to come lose any moment. The glittering red *saree*, with a clutch and the diamond jewellery, made her look like some movie star. The red really suited her. I had never seen her in Indian clothes and this was a welcome change. She looked nice and I felt guilty that I had not complimented her!

'Why would I hate you?'

'Last night in college and I drag you out here.'

We had driven to a creek near our college that had served as our drinking place for quite some time. Not a soul was around. Shashank, Mittal and I used to come here quite often before Haryana police picked us up a few times on our way back and until we got tired of paying bribes to get out of those situations. It was an unfinished bridge and had been cordoned off years ago after a couple of bikers had drowned in the water below.

I walked Malini to the edge and we sat there, our feet hanging from the edge of the bridge. Silence engulfed us. Except for the crickets, bugs, the wind blowing through the weeds and the water gushing beneath our feet. The moon peeked from behind the clouds and reflected off the water beneath us. The redness of the Malini's lips still shined through all the darkness. Her eyes sparkled.

'You don't have to be sorry. I had no one else there in college. So I don't mind.' She picked up a stone and threw it across the creek. 'By the way, it also means that I had just one person to impress today. But you don't seem to care . . .'

'Aw! You look stunning!'

'It means nothing now,' she said.

'I would have drooled! Just that I was a little caught up,' I said, trying to make it better. I looked at her once again. She looked amazing. Moreover, I had never seen someone bare so much, navel, oodles of cleavage, a flat stomach . . . and not look vulgar, so she was a treat to look at!

'Thank you,' she said. As much as she tried not to smile, a hint of it came across her face. I kept looking at her smile, those eyes, and I could think of was Avantika. I wished she were there. My eyes welled up. I missed her. I really did. Everything had ceased to make sense without her.

'What happened?' she asked me.

'I just wished she was there this night. We had gone through this night like a zillion times before . . . we never thought this would end like this . . .'

Malini pulled and made me sit closer to her on the edge of the creek. 'Never mind,' she said. 'Things will be fine.'

'I hope so,' I said, wistfully.

'Do you have something to drink in your car?' she asked.

'I did pick up something from the party, I guess. Didn't really see what it was.'

'Let's get drunk and make out, what say?' she smiled wickedly. 'After all, I do look smashing today, right?' She desperately tried to lift my fucked-up mood.

'Err . . . what?'

'Just kidding! Let's just do the first part,' she laughed out aloud.

I left her at the creek and rummaged through all the clothes, books and newspapers that had accumulated on the back seat of the car. Since there was no Avantika, there was no one to ask me to clean up the car. I looked for the bottle I had thrown in. There was champagne and an unfinished bottle of vodka.

'We have this,' I raised both the bottles in the air as I walked towards her.

'Not bad. Let me see.' She read out the brand of the champagne. 'This will put you to sleep for the rest of the night.'

'What do you mean?' I asked.

'I mean we all know how much you can take. It is not a secret anymore.'

'Is it? You are no better. No offence, but we have seen too how you behave when you are drunk.' I smirked. 'I still remember Mumbai.'

'I will give you that.'

We both laughed.

She popped open the champagne bottle and took a huge swig at it. 'Not bad.' She handed over the bottle to me.

I gulped a little. 'Nice.'

It was sweet. Malini was being sweeter.

'Our lives are so screwed up,' she said.

We had gotten drunk, and though we sat in the car to drive back to college, we could not. I was seeing things in twins and even triplets. She had never driven a car with gears, so we were stuck there until the time I could have driven. We flattened our seats, kicked open the doors and decided to catch a little rest before we would go back.

'I know,' I said and held her hand.

'Why isn't there a sun roof in your car?' she said looking up.

'I should get one.'

'At least I could have seen the stars,' she said and ran her fingers on my face.

'You can see me instead of the stars,' I said.

'You go and see Avantika.'

'She is never coming back . . . she is history . . .' I said and held her hand tighter.

'She will never be.'

'I am history for her . . .'

'That can never be,' she said.

'Why are we talking about her? Let's talk about us.'

'There is nothing to talk about us,' she said, stiffening up a little.

'Why? Had she not been around, I would have definitely asked you out!'

'*Had she* . . . Anyway, I think I would have rather gone out with Mittal than you! . . . but then we could have gone out, you know,' she said, looked at me and smiled.

'Could have? We still can Malini.'

'I can't fight with memories of Avantika. And you wouldn't be able to . . . memories of him,' she said wistfully, looked at me. We did not exchange a word. She looked at a distance. We were quiet. Time passed and she just lay there in my arms and said nothing.

'Thinking of him?' I asked finally.

'Thinking of us,' she said.

I wished I had a sunroof. *If I'd only known* . . .

We Move Apart, We Come Closer

After college ended, I was one of the few students who had a three-month break before joining the firm I had been placed in. Many of my classmates had already joined their firms. Shashank had moved out to Bangalore for his Investment bank job. Mittal had joined the Mumbai office of his company. Avantika too had left for Mumbai. *The farewell night.*

'Nice place!' I said. 'Isn't it a little empty?'

'I know. It's a little too big for me. But I will fill it up,' she said as she sat on of the cardboard boxes.

'So how was Canada?' I asked her.

Malini had left for Canada the day after the farewell night for fifteen days. But she was back in town and she had called me. I had been waiting for her call!

'It was good,' she said. 'I met old friends, relatives . . . it was fun!'

'Broke up?'

'We were never together, but yes, broken up.'

'So any post-break up depression?' I asked her.

'Not really . . . it is okay. I have moved on,' she said as she ripped open one of the cardboard boxes and looked for something in it.

'See.' She handed me a bunch of photographs.

'Aha . . . nice! I don't know how long it has been to see photographs like this,' I said while I went over the pictures. 'Nice.' I handed the bundle back to them.

'So Deb, what's on the Avantika front?' She asked.

'We have moved on. She has stopped messaging or calling. Just one odd message a day. She is fine with herself I guess. Kabir is there too . . . so maybe they are together. I don't know and I don't want to know. Why are we talking about her again? I have moved on too.'

'Okay, we won't . . . so what else?'

'Boring days . . . and yea . . . missed you.'

'Where are you putting up?'

'Remember Nitin? With him . . . He leaves for office early morning and I pretty much have nothing to do,' I said.

'I remember him . . . Anyway, Any plans for the day?'

'I am very busy, Malini. I have to go back home, log in to FB and play angry birds all day long,' I said sarcastically.

'Very funny . . . Help me unpack?' She made such a puppy face, that I could not say no. Also, I had nothing to do. I just did not have a life.

'Sure.'

For the next three hours we meticulously unpacked each one of the thirty huge cardboard boxes stuffed with everything from clothes, to mantelpieces, from books to bundles of pictures like the ones I just saw. We crushed the boxes and pushed them down the garbage chute.

'Malini?'

'Yes?'

'I think you need some furniture,' I said. 'People generally like to sit and sleep . . . but then, entirely your choice . . .' I mocked.

'Very funny,' she said.

The house was beautiful, but it was bare. Apart from the two beds in the two rooms, the cupboards and a sofa in the living room, the house was empty. No study tables, no chairs and nowhere to put all the stuff she had carried to that place!

'Whose house is this anyway?' I asked her as we boarded the auto to *Panchkuiya*, the furniture market. She had requested me to come along and I could not say no. The last fifteen days had been super boring and this was a welcome change.

'My *maasi* used to live here before they moved to Canada. They want to keep it as an investment, so I am using it!'

'Good for you.'

'Good for them too. An occupied house is always well maintained,' she said coldly.

The auto driver zipped through the streets of Connaught place and we reached the market, lined with furniture shops of all shapes and sizes.

'Bas Bhaiya!' She tapped the auto driver's shoulder to make him stop.

'So what all are we looking for?'

'Study table first,' she said and led me into a small furniture shop.

We spent the entire day choosing, haggling and buying furniture of all shapes and sizes. I had absolutely no design sense so I had kept quiet for most part of it. I was visibly impressed at her decisiveness. Within a few hours, she had picked out a couple of study tables, a few chairs, a few stools that I had no idea where she would put, a few lamps and other pieces of furniture that seemed pretty useless and strange.

'I have no idea where you would put so much stuff!' I said, as it seemed she would not stop buying stuff.

'Deb, shut up. They all fit in.'

'Fine with me! It is your house!'

'Let's go,' she said.

'Where?'

'Sarojini Nagar!' she said.

'Sarojini? Why? I thought we bought everything, didn't we?'

'Nope.'

'So what is left?'

'Cushions. Mattresses. Bed sheets. Curtains. Bed sheets. Towels. Some other small things!'

I liked the excitement in her voice. I guess it was a girl thing - doing up their own place. I smiled at her and she smiled back. After fifteen days, I was finally happy again.

'This is a long day,' I said. It was a nice day too.

'It sure is,' she grabbed my hand and led to another auto and we headed towards Sarojini Nagar.

The place teemed with girls of every shape and size, jostling for space. The place probably had everything that a girl can ask for. Things were cheap and fake but they did not seem to care. Everyone had huge bags in their hands and within ten minutes, I had three of them in my hands too!

She frantically flitted from one shop to another and picked up everything that she could lay her hands on. She seemed to buy everything that one could possibly buy: everything that could be haggled for - Curtains. Bed sheets. Cushions. Mugs. Crockery. *Everything!*

Occasionally, she stopped to look for clothes for herself, bangles and the like but other than that, she was pretty focused. We missed lunch and had something filthy on the road. It was filling, and that is the best I can say about it.

'Please tell me if we are done?' I asked. I was exhausted. I had nodded my approval for things she wasn't sure about and carried her bags all morning!

'Yes. Finally.' She smiled.

'Going now?'

'Sure!' she said. She still did not look tired! *Where the hell did she get her energy from?* I must have dozed off in the auto because I remember waking up to a screaming Malini. She was shouting on the phone on a furniture dealer who said that their guy would be a few hours late.

'Chill Malini,' I croaked.

'Oh . . . you woke up? Sorry for that.'

'It is okay.'

'Thank You, Deb,' she said and pulled my cheeks.

'For?'

'For helping me with the shopping . . . I wouldn't have been able to do this alone.'

I looked outside. The sun had set and it was evening already.

'I did nothing,' I said groggily.

'You did enough,' she said, 'Go back to sleep.' She put my head on her shoulder and run her hand over my face. As I dozed off, I heard her whisper to herself, *'I missed you.'*

'It's good to be back,' she said as she hugged me.

It had been a long and tiring day. We had spent the last four hours doing up her place and we did a great job! Her place suddenly looked warm and inviting. It reminded me of her *old* hostel room.

I was tired. I could not remember the last time I had worked so hard. We had cleaned the house inside out, shifted and set the tables and chairs in all possible combinations until she was satisfied. We tried out all permutations for curtains until she said *yes*.

We filled up the cupboards. It was the most interesting part of the day as I got to rummage through her exotic lingerie! I was *impressed*.

Unlike the movies, where couples have a great time unpacking and end up making out in the end, nothing of that sort happened. It was boring affair.

'Are we done for sure? Or is there still something you don't like?'

'Aw! No, it's done! It looks nice, doesn't it?' she smiled and looked around. I agreed with her. It looked like a cozy little place, far from the barren empty flat it was that morning. She had stuffed it with so much wood and textile that it indeed looked very nice.

'You are good!'

'So are you,' she said and pulled my cheeks.

'But isn't this house a little too big for just you?' I asked her. 'You should look for roommate.'

'What do you want to say?'

'I mean . . . get a roommate. I mean, it will be nice time pass and plus the extra money you can earn through rent!' I said and realized that money was never an issue for Malini.

'Oh . . .'

'What happened?' I asked

'I thought something else,' she said and the enthusiasm in her voice dipped.

'What?'

'Leave it.'

'Tell me.'

'It is nothing,' she said as she rearranged the cushions *again*.

'Tell me!'

'I just thought you were referring to yourself,' she sighed.

'Myself?'

'Yeah . . .'

'Oh . . . myself! Roommate?'

There was an awkward silence. Neither of us said anything. We just stood there and looked at each other. Three days later, I moved in. Initially, she was excited but later she advised me against it. *Why?* It would not be good for Avantika and me, *the relationship*. I told her there was nothing left to save in the relationship. I disregarded every plea of hers of not to move in and invited myself to live there. Deep inside, I knew her pleas of asking me to stay away were only half-hearted.

Life Gets Better

'Did you call her?' she asked as she entered the flat.

'Nope,' I said as I switched the channel.

'Deb? Why didn't you?'

'I didn't feel like it,' I said as I turned up the volume to drown her voice out.

'We need to talk,' she said and closed the door of her room behind her.

Malini had no problems with me staying put there. At least in the past few months, she had not shown an iota of displeasure with me being there. In fact, she was fun roommate!

'So?' Malini said as she came out of her room in stringy top and hot pants. I told you—*fun* roommate! I had seen her in lesser clothes in the past two months, in her exotic lingerie to be precise. She grabbed the remote from me and turned the volume down.

'So? What?' I said.

No matter how much I acted, I had still not moved on. The days used to kill me. The evenings and nights were easier because Malini was around. The last thing I wanted from Malini was to bug me with what used to haunt me every single minute of the day—*Avantika*.

'Deb, why don't you do something about it? I cannot see you like this. Why don't you just talk to her?' she asked.

'I am not as bad and miserable as you are making out me to be. I am a lot better!'

'Yeah, maybe! But you need to do something fast. I cannot date until the time I have a male roommate. You know how people talk,' she said and chuckled.

'Why do you need to date? I am here! Date *me*.'

'Naah! You are not boyfriend material,' she said.

'Seriously, Is there a problem because I am staying here?' I asked, trying out a puppy face expression.

It worked. She snuggled up to me on the couch and said, 'Yes, a little. I do not want to get used to you. It is already happening and it scares me.'

'What's the harm if it's happening?' I asked.

Over the last few months, Malini had become the most important person in my life. Slowly and steady, she knew all about me. She had taken good care of me! Often, she reminded me of Avantika because before Malini, she was the only person who had cared for me that much!

I was a mess when I first shifted in with Malini. I did not wash clothes, threw clothes around, did not know a thing to cook, and yet she put up with all that for two months. Lately things were changing, as I involved myself in household chores, and it was not because she asked me to do so . . . but because I wanted to help Malini out. Thank her for what she did for me. Even after a long day in office, she would insist to do everything for me.

Sometimes, it scared both of us! She was a little too committed to see me happy.

Was I falling in love again? No, I was *not.*

But I was sure that Malini had feelings for me and that is what scared me the most. After all what she had done for me, I did not want to break her heart. Three weeks after I moved in, we had decided that we would sleep in different rooms. The late night 'hug-and-talk' sessions often used to end up in awkward silences and sometimes, sex. We had made out thrice in that period. All three of those nights were followed by awkward mornings.

We managed to stick to our rule for a week. However, after that we started sleeping on the couch and even talked to each other on the phone from different rooms.

Interestingly, we had made out just thrice in the two months that I had spent in her flat. We were drunk twice.

It was hard not to slip . . . you cannot blame me, her after-office clothes were as skimpy as they could have gotten. It was miracle enough that I managed to keep my hands off her for the majority of the time. Moreover, I was single. There was nothing wrong in what I did. Who knew, maybe Avantika was doing the same with Kabir?

That day, things got a little awkward again. Malini was a sweet person and it was hard not to like her.

'You don't love me,' she said. 'I will always be a rebound.'

'Do you love me?' I asked her.

'I care about you,' she said and ran her hands over my shirt. 'I am stopping myself from falling for you. I would have been in love with you. Maybe, I already am. But *this* can't be . . .'

'Why love *me*? I am a loser,' I asked.

'Wish I could answer that. But tomorrow you are calling her up,' she said.

'Why are you pushing me towards her? Maybe it's you I want to be with?'

'Didn't I tell you? I cannot compete with her. I am not that strong. And I know you will be the happiest with her,' she said. 'And seriously, I can't take your crying Deb. Not only does it look silly, and . . . stupid. It hurts.'

'What do I tell her? I mean, I don't think Avantika even thinks about me that much.'

'You know that can't be. She loves you more than anything!'

'She doesn't call me, she doesn't message me anymore. It is only I who calls her now. I am sick of it and I am sure she is with that bastard now.'

'Why do you say that?'

'She doesn't text or call me anymore! *Why?*'

'Deb . . . I don't blame her,' she said.

'Why? Because you are a girl and you must have some stupid reason to back her, don't you?'

'She gave you enough chances Deb. She begged for more than two months. She put up with everything you said to her . . . the taunt, the abuses, the angry tones. What else do you want her to take? She just assumed you would never come back,' she said.

'Never come back? Is that why I call her every five days? To never come back?'

'Have you ever tried to talk to her calmly and not bring up Kabir in your conversations? Have *you?* Have you tried to understand what she has been going through? Deb, do not fool yourself. I know you stay up nights and read her old messages. Cry. Think. Ponder . . . Then why this Deb? Just because she made out with a guy she doesn't love? You have made out with me! We have had sex, for heavens' sake, but you love her . . . and you love her like crazy. Nothing is going to change that. It will always stay in your heart and it will keep killing you unless you don't do anything about it.'

'But—'

'But what Deb? Stop this foolishness now. Go to her. It's Avantika. She is your *baby!* Look what you have reduced her to! Why did you do this to her Deb?'

'She is just fine . . .'

'Call her tomorrow and ask her if she's fine!' she said, broke out of my embrace and slammed the door behind her as she entered her room. I sat there reflecting on what she said. There was desperation and love in her voice.

Avantika? She was not really the same now. Who said that? Was Malini the same? She was *not.* I felt bad about myself. I was hurting the people I loved the most. I got up and walked towards her room and was about to knock when I heard her crying inside. It had to do with me. I knocked and entered.

'Are you crying?' I asked.

'Silly question,' she said and wiped her tears. I went and sat next to her. She put her hands across me.

'Try this. Don't blame me if it isn't good enough,' I said. I had made pasta for her that evening, but I could not tell her because she picked the *Avantika issue* so soon.

'Not bad. Impressive indeed!' she said as she ate.

'I am learning a few things from you!' I smiled.

'Do you have a sadistic agenda of making all the awesome girls around you cry?' she said, still crying.

'I never said you are awesome.'

'I *wish* I was.'

'Aw! You are the awesom*est* ever!' I said and hugged her.

'Deb, I have longed for a guy who would love me like you love her. At times, I wanted to be *her.* And had I been a complete bitch, I would have stopped you from going back to her.'

'Why don't you stop me?'

'You belong to *her.*'

'Umm.'

There was an awkward silence.

'Call her tomorrow,' she said.

'Give me a week.'

'A week it is,' she said and hugged me.

'Deb?'

'Yes?'

She held me close; I could her breath on my lips. She said, 'I want to say something to you.'

'What?' I asked.

'Don't answer to what I am going to say. I just want to say this because if I don't, I will never be able to forgive myself,' she said and the tears in her eye reappeared.

'I won't,' I said. 'What is it?

She put a finger on my lips and said, 'Deb, Please don't go . . . I want you to stay,' she whispered in my ears. She closed her eyes and hugged me.

The last two months had been good. They could have been a lot worse. She had saved me. I did not leave her that night. I would never be able to pay back what Malini had done for me. She was an angel.

Malini was bedridden since the last three days. No matter what I said, she blamed me the pasta for it.

'Don't get up. I will get that,' I said as she tried to reach for the thermometer.

It had been three days and the fever had started to subside. *Just a viral infection*, the doctor said. No food poisoning, I told her, but she would not budge. She still blamed the pasta.

It was a strange feeling to take care of someone, as usually it was the other way round. People used to take care of me!

'You are very sweet, Deb,' she said.

'Me? Why?'

'I can never imagine a guy doing what you are doing!'

'Ahh . . . c'mon . . . I did not do nothing,' I said and blushed

'Yes, you didn't.' She hugged me. 'You did *nothing* . . .'

I put her to sleep. She was *cute*.

Of Mittal's Woes!

'Mittal called today,' I said.

It had been more than a week and I had not yet called Avantika. Malini had recovered from the viral and she gifted me a new watch as a token of thanks for taking care of her. Even though she could, I could not have repaid Malini back for what she had done for me. No amount of watches or jewellery could repay that debt. She had done a lot for me.

'How is Mittal doing?'

'Good.'

'First time after college?'

'Naah . . . we have talked about five or six times,' I said.

'Best friends, huh?' she winked. 'What did he say?'

'Nothing much. He is coming to Delhi next week and might stay with us.'

'Deb, can you pass on that jug,' she said. 'That would be nice. How long would he be here?'

'Not very long. A day or two.'

'You don't seem excited,' she said as she served breakfast.

Malini was a great cook! Since she was a health freak, we did not use to go out and eat junk a lot those days. She was happy whipping up something new for us every weekend. She even tried to take me out jogging, but I couldn't wake up that early!

'Obviously I am excited,' I said. I was *not* excited but yes, I was looking forward to it. It had been long since I met him.

'Umm . . . you know what, Deb?'

'What?'

'Those three days that I was bedridden?'

'What about those?' I asked.

'Those were the best three days I had spent in the longest time!' she said and smiled at me. I blushed.

'Were they?' I asked.

'They were so nice! You used to sit by the chair and hold my hand, stay up all night just in case I needed anything! I loved the way you took care of me, made me go to sleep, made me laugh and tried to make it all better . . . I should probably pay you and keep you here,' she said and voice trailed off.

'Hmm,' I couldn't say anything.

'. . . And I would just hate to snatch all *this* from someone . . . anyone,' she said wistfully.

'Are you serious you don't have a crush on Mittal?' I joked.

It had been three hours that morning that she had working continuously to clean the flat. She had taken a half day from office just to do that! It is strange how quickly time flies. From cleaning up the hostel room, every time a girl was supposed to walk in, to cleaning up a house. We all grow up.

'Yes, I do. Remember that date, Mittal and I, since then,' she said and winked. 'He is awesome!'

'Oh . . . good for you.'

'I wish that my crush on him would have made you jealous.'

'Oh, it sure did!' I said.

I liked the *devil-may-care* Malini more. She should *not* have told me that she had strong feelings for me. At least I would have felt a lot less guilty then. And a lot less confused. Malini had done nothing to drive me away unlike Avantika and she had done a lot for me, selflessly.

Malini had an elaborate menu ready for this *asshole*. It almost looked like we were married couple expecting a guest. There was bang on the door accompanied by a huge shout. It was Mittal for sure.

'Hey!' he shouted and hugged me. He had changed. The sedentary office job had made him *fat*. The abs were gone, he told me.

'Are you losing hair?' Malini said and they hugged.

'You look good together,' he said.

'Umm . . . we are not together,' she said.

'But you guys are making out right?' He laughed. It was still the same Mittal we had known!

'This is for you two.' He handed over a carton of beer bottles. 'Nice house by the way!'

Malini thanked him for it.

'So what is going on these days?' he asked us.

'I am slogging my ass off . . . and he is getting fatter by the day,' Malini said.

We all had a laugh at my expense. For those moments, we were back in college!

'So you actually live here?' he asked me.

'Yes . . . I mean, just a temporary thing till I leave for the job.'

'That I know . . . but this is where you live?' he asked again.

'Yes. Why?' Malini asked.

'No, I mean . . . is the Avantika chapter closed?' he asked.

'Not really. He will patch up in a few days,' Malini said. 'Anyway, you two continue with your male bonding thing. I have to leave for office.'

'Bye,' we echoed.

'Is that what you wear to office?' Mittal asked and pointed to the short skirt that Malini wore that day.

'Yes, why?' she asked.

'Is there a vacancy in your office?' he said and winked at her.

'You have not changed,' she smiled. 'Bye Deb. I will be late,' she said, kissed me on the cheek and left. Mittal saw that and I saw the expression on his face change. Ideally, 'the college Mittal' would have given me a high five, but this Mittal, he gave a sceptical look to me.

Malini called later that evening that and told us she would be late and bid Mittal goodbye. Mittal was not staying over for the night. He told me everything about his new job and said he missed his college days like hell. He was *not* happy! He had just bought a new car and new place but he said nothing would beat the bike rides and the tiny hostel room. I concurred. We drank and discussed every tiny detail of our college lives! At the end of it, we were drunk.

'You two have a slight thing going, isn't that true?' he said.

'Nope. She has feelings for me, but then she says I need to go back to her.'

'What do *you* think?'

'Malini, I mean, she is an awesome person. But I would always be unfair to her and she knows that. I would never forget Avantika, and even she has made me realize this repeatedly. But, who knows! I might just get over Avantika someday. Then, Malini and I—'

'I think you should shift as soon as possible,' he said solemnly. I had never seen him so serious.

'Are you alright? I thought you would ask me to go out and sleep with her every night!' I joked.

'If a girl sleeps with any guy for more than four times, she will fall in love with him!' he said and his voice cracked.

'Mittal? *What* are you saying?'

'Yeah . . .'

'Is everything fine?'

'Nothing is fine man,' he said as he got up and took a huge swig at his bottle.

'Tell me.'

'She got married last week man.'

'She?'

'Nidhi.'

'Nidhi? Who?'

'You don't know her,' he said.

I was actually getting uncomfortable seeing him talk like this.

'I know that I don't know her,' I said. 'Wait! Is this is the girl you used to talk to in MDI? Oh . . . tell me everything. From the start!'

'I broke up with her when I came to MDI,' he said and his eyes were wet. Maybe, Shashank and I were right. He was hiding something.

'So?' I said.

'I broke up for no reason. She was getting too close to me. Things were getting serious and I chickened out. I went away. I did not have the courage to take the final step! I was so young,' he said and held his head. He almost cried now.

'So this was the girl you talked to? I do not understand. What happened?'

'I loved her but her parents started looking for a guy for her marriage. They asked her if she had a boyfriend, I asked her to say no. She wanted to get married to me, but I did not know whether I could be with her *forever*. I didn't know that losing her would affect me so much.'

'But didn't you have other girlfriends?'

'I did. I was trying to run from the fact that I loved her. I wished I hadn't.'

'Why didn't you do anything about it?'

'I tried. After she was engaged, I realized what a fool I had been. I told my parents and they thought I was crazy. But they slowly understood that I was serious about her. It was already too late. She said she couldn't leave the guy she was engaged to. She gave me a million chances and I had let all of them go waste. Not a day passed in college when she didn't ask me if we could be back together. She waited for two long years. I was a fool.'

'What did she say later?'

'What would she say? She made her parents wait for two years. Now, that things were in place for her wedding, what could she have done? I asked her to come, run with me, but she said it would be unfair to her parents. I do not blame her. I was at fault. I was so fucking wrong man . . . I should have listened to Shashank.'

'Shashank knew?'

'Yes.'

'Why didn't you tell me?'

'You were not in a state to be told anything like this. You had your own problems,' he said.

'Who else knows?'

'Avantika,' he said.

'Avantika? *What?* When did you tell her?'

'I have met her couple of times. She lives near my office in Mumbai. Bandra.'

'Anyway, we talk about that later. So what happened?'

'What? Nothing man. I am just *ruined.* What else,' he said and smiled.

'Are you fine?'

'I am fine. I will just go, screw a few girls, end up alone and die.' He smiled again. 'I hate to say this, but I miss her. Maybe, I will get over her someday, but right now, it kills me.'

It hurt to see him like this.

He continued, 'You know what? We are all assholes. We will look at everywhere else, and we don't look where we should really look. I mean, she was right there all the time. I mean, are we so fucking selfish? I slept with countless women and she never raised an eyebrow. She never said anything to me. All she wanted was that I should go back to her.'

'Hmm. It will be okay.' I did not know what to say.

'Deb, I am losing my sleep. To think of her with another guy is killing me. I should have been *that* guy. I gave it all away! I didn't deserve her. Maybe, it is for her own good. I am sure her husband would love her,' he said and shut up.

Tears streaked down his face and he looked away. Love brings great men to their knees; Mittal was no different. We did not say a word. I am sure we were both thinking about the love of our lives - Nidhi and Avantika.

I did not want to end up like Mittal. I had seen Avantika with another guy and it was sheer torture. Suddenly, I wanted to be with her. I wanted to have her in my life and never let her go. Mittal had scared me. Mittal was stronger than me, if he was going through so much pain, I could only imagine how I would react!

What if Avantika finds another guy and I become just another ex-boyfriend in her life. It was a scary thought. I *needed* Avantika.

Mittal left that day, with a smile on his face as he always did. But this time I could see what was behind that smile. *Regret*. Regret that he would find hard to shake off.

He told me about Shashank too. Shashank had called me a few times over the last few months but I had ignored his calls. After the break-up, I had lost interest in anything around me.

Anyway, Mittal told me that Shashank was trying to convince his parents for the wedding. He had already handled matters at Geetika's end. As per Mittal, Shashank would manage everything. Mittal was rarely ever wrong. Except the one time with himself.

'What did he say?' Malini asked as she served dinner.

'Nothing much,' I said as I dug into the *parantha*. I was visibly disturbed after seeing Mittal. I was scared and it showed on face. I was crapping my pants.

'It is okay, if you don't want to talk about it, but I know what is bothering you.' She walked away from the dining table and sat on the sofa.

'What?'

'Avantika . . . What if she finds another guy,' she said as a matter of fact.

'It isn't that,' I said. *How the fuck does she know everything?*

'Yes. Sure it isn't,' she said sarcastically.

Malini sounded pissed. She had her reasons. I was with her, but not really with her. How hard could it have been for Malini, I don't know. I never will.

But Malini?

Why would a girl like her fall for me? Anyway, I tried to steer the topic away from Avantika and talk about something else though it really didn't work. I just shut up and ate. Soon after, Malini said she was sleepy and went to her room.

Needless to say, neither she could sleep nor I. I knocked her door.

'May I?'

'Yes,' she said. She was reading a book.

'I thought you were sleepy.'

'I was,' she said and flopped closed the book. She didn't look happy all evening. I had gone to her room to make her feel a little better. She was all I had.

'Malini?'

'Yes?' she said.

'If Avantika wasn't there . . . We would have been,' I said and stopped midway.

'Deb? You think I am sad because of her?'

'Are you not?'

'No! It's not her. It's just that . . . you will leave in a few days. You will join your job and I will be all alone,' she said, wistfully.

'Hmm . . .'

'It will be tough for me you know.'

'It will be tough for me too,' I said.

She continued, 'I have gotten so used to seeing you around. Just thinking that this place would have just me in it makes me sick in the stomach. You know, coming back from office and not seeing you, not seeing the mess around you, not bugging you to go take a bath, forcing food down your throat. I will miss all this.'

'Get a roommate,' I said when I should have hugged her. I wanted to hug her.

'It will not be the same. They don't make cute guys anymore.'

'I am cute?'

'The best I have seen,' she said, put her hands around me and pecked me. 'I am so spoilt now.'

'You? What on earth have I even done to spoil you? I am the spoilt one here!'

'You have done nothing. But I guess people just get too used to the idea of *you*. And the idea of you is brilliant, Deb . . .'

'You are being too—'

'Shut up.'

'If you say so.'

She clung on to me. 'I will miss you,' she said.

'I will miss you too. And I will come and visit often.'

'That you know will never happen,' she said. 'And it should not.'

'It will. I can't live without you.'

'Thank you. You are being so—'

'Shut up . . .'

I kept her hugged until she dozed off. I left her seeing her sleep like a baby. It was one of those days when you ask yourself, 'What have I done to deserve this?'

I rarely thanked God for anything those days. But I did that day, for giving me Malini.

While she slept peacefully, my mind became a battleground of conflicts. Malini and I. Was there was a possibility? She was the sunshine that shone on me when there was darkness all around. I liked her being around. She was the only good part of my life!

What would it be like, not to have her around? I shuddered to think. I tried not to.

Of When I Don't Want to Leave

'You eventually have to pack!' she said.

Over the past week she had been saying this over and again. I had been delaying it for as long as possible. My going away would have seemed real had I started packing.

I wanted it to be an illusion and not accept it for as long as possible!

I did not want that to happen soon. I loved this life. This life was good. Being alone would be crazy and depressing. I had gotten used to living with Malini.

That was why I was avoiding packing. It would have driven home the fact that I will have to leave in a few days. I was still living in denial and I did *not* want to go. The fact that I would be entering an empty flat without Malini sucked.

A new city where I will have to build a life of my own from scratch was not exciting. It was saddening and depressing.

Malini and I had been going shopping every day for essentials. Bed sheets. Blankets. Everything that she thought I would not be interested in buying on my own and would start living without them. But more often than not, we ended up shopping for each other. In the last week itself I gifted her two perfumes, three pairs of footwear and some other small things that I don't remember. *Seven days.* Just seven days and I will be miles away from her. The time I had spent with her would be history. I felt *sad*.

'I will. There is still time! Seven days. It will hardly take one day to pack everything! Moreover, we are not wasting your sick leaves in packing.'

Malini had taken the week off since it was the last one with me. I loved her for doing that. I wanted her to do so. I told her that this would make it harder for both of us, but she did not listen. She wanted time with me and so did I. We wanted to make the most of the time we had.

'Come here,' I said.

She came to the couch and held me close. We had spent hours in the past few days like that.

'Deb?' she said. 'Now that I won't be there to distract you, mend it with her.'

'She doesn't care. No calls, no messages even now.'

'But you do! You are miserable without her and you will be even more miserable when I won't be around.'

'I will come to visit you. You make it all better, won't you? I need *you*.'

'Everyday?'

'As if I could be with her every day!'

'It is not the same. She can be around you even when she is not. I can't.'

'You are underestimating what you mean to me.'

'No, I am not,' she said and clung on to me harder. I thought she would cry out but she did not. I was sure she cried in her heart.

'Why do you keep pushing me towards her? *Maybe* I don't want to go.'

'If it was to happen with you and me, I would have sold my soul for that to happen,' she smiled and kissed me.

Maybe *this* was what was meant to be! I didn't have to leave her.

'I know you love this place,' Malini said. She had booked us a place at the most ridiculously expensive resort some fifty kilometres off Delhi. It was a huge fortress lit in the most fascinating styles. Pools. Huge banquets with dinosaur sized chandeliers. Staff who could be passed as models. Buffets that served everything that you might have ever eaten. Even at thirty thousand a night, this place was worth it!

'I don't love this place. I have never been here! I just have heard about it . . . and this is so awesome!'

'I knew you would like it,' she said. It was Malini's farewell gift to me.

'But you shouldn't have spent so much. Had you gone totally nuts! Thirty thousand?'

'How did you know?'

'I checked the price listings,' I said and she smiled.

'Don't worry about it!' she said and clung on to my arm as we walked past a pool, and picked up a wine glass each on our way.

'Are we going to have sex today?' I asked.

'You want to?'

'It would be a shame to waste a room which costs that much!'

'Oh the room? That's why you want to do it? I thought it

was something to do with me,' she punched.

'Obviously, it has to do with you! Or I would have a random girl for it!' I smiled and added, 'Who wouldn't want to sleep with you!'

'Oh yeah?'

'Sure. Let's do it.'

'We will see,' she said.

I had asked the question in good humour but the fact that she had not totally shot it down had me in tingles. We were not even drunk! Somehow, that night I wanted to make out with Malini. I blamed it on the overwhelming emotion that flowed that day. It was our *last* day together!

'Ain't the food just awesome?' I told her as we found ourselves a huge comfortable couch near the pool. The table in front of us had loads of food.

'Yes it is.'

'Why are you starving yourself then?' I asked.

'I just don't feel like it,' she said.

'Hmm . . .' I kept the plate aside and held her hand.

'Last night together, Deb,' she murmured.

'Why? We have tomorrow night?'

'You have a flight.'

'It is 2am! We have the whole night,' I reasoned.

'It's 2pm stupid. Only God knows what you will do there alone?'

'I will be fine. Moreover, I will call you every day! So you can guide me all the time!'

'If you insist,' she said solemnly.

'Don't be sad Malini. I told you, I will be around . . . We will call, message, you are always on Google talk or Facebook and so am I. It will not be so bad. We can fly down to meet each once a month . . . even twice a month. We can afford it!'

'I don't know. Just take care of yourself over there. I will be so worried about you,' she said.

'C'mon, don't be such a mom!'

'Shut up . . . and don't spend days without bathing.'

'Will you stop that already?'

'Okay . . . just one last thing . . . Please, please shave on your first day at office. I will call to check.'

'Okay mom,' I said.

We both laughed . . . which was more like a desperate one. That laugh was supposed to hide the sadness that we will not be together anymore.

'I had a nice time with you, Deb. I really did. This was *not* really a relationship but whatever we had, whatever it was . . . it was beautiful! I just wish . . . it could have lasted.' She smiled.

'Whatever we *have*,' I corrected her.

'We will see.'

'Nothing has ended Malini. I am still around.'

Just then, I heard a male voice shout out behind my back. 'DEB?'

I looked around. It was *him*. Kabir.

'Hey! Malini? You guys? Here!' he cried out loud.

Bastard, I murmured and Malini hit me.

'Hi Kabir,' she said.

'Hi,' I said.

'What you doing here?' he asked.

'We come here often., Malini said. 'You?'

Kabir missed the sarcasm in her voice.

'I have an office trip here. So what are you guys up to?'

The minute he said it, my mind went into convulsions as to whether even Avantika was around. I looked behind to quickly glance through his office group. Nope.

Maybe she was in her room. Maybe she had not come altogether. What if she is here and had seen me with Malini? But then she already knows that I am living with Malini? And Kabir? Maybe they have put up in one room? Is that where she is? Should I go talk to her? No, I should not. I should wait.

'Why don't you join us?' Malini asked him much to my displeasure. *Why on earth did she do that?*

'Sure.'

To make things worse he could not even refuse. As soon as he sat down, much to my chagrin, he started with his small talk. He asked what we were up to those days.

'I am working with HUL and he is leaving for his office in a few days.' Malini said.

'Oh . . . where are they sending you?' He asked me.

'Bangalore.'

'So you have been living here? In Delhi?'

'Yes,' we echoed.

'We live together,' I said. I know why I said that. I wanted Avantika to know. Hurt her. If at all, it mattered to her. *Why?* I didn't know. To tell her, that I was doing fine. Kabir would obviously tell her.

'Where were you posted? Mumbai I guess?' I asked him.

'Yes. Though I often shuttle between Delhi and Mumbai.'

'Oh cool!' I said. I wanted to kick him into the water with weights tied to his ankles.

'So what else?' I asked him. Obviously, I wanted to get something about Avantika out. I just had to know. I prepared myself for the worst—*We are going out, we will get married in a few days!*

'Nothing much. You tell me. What are you up to?'

'Usual boring corporate life,' Malini butted in. 'Avantika is in the same office right?'

'Yes, but I have never seen her in Mumbai. She is in a different branch so that's in another office at the other end of the city,' he said.

'I thought you would know,' he said and looked at me.

'They don't talk anymore,' Malini said.

'Oh . . . I am sorry,' he said.

It is because of you asshole!

'So when was the last time you talked to her?' Malini asked.

'I don't know . . . just before leaving college, I guess?'

'And never after that?' I asked.

'Yes . . . but why?' Kabir asked, a little puzzled because of the questions we threw at him.

'Nothing, just generally,' she said.

Someone from his office group shouted out his name.

'Need to go,' he said. 'Nice meeting you after such a long time. Catch you later.'

We all got up, hugged and he left. And following that there was an awkward silence.

'He hasn't talked to her after the college ended,' she said.

My head was bursting with possibilities and I did not want to talk about it anymore. Anyway, just the sight of that guy made me sick in the stomach. It was anyway hard enough to quit visiting his Facebook profile for signs of Avantika.

'How does it matter?' I said, a little pissed off, a little relieved.

'Can we order these things in the room too?'

'Yes.'

'And a movie too?' It was stupid question since the screen in our room was thrice the size of the biggest television I had ever seen. 'And lots of alcohol?' I winked.

'Are you planning to get naughty?' she smirked.

'Could be!'

'I don't mind,' she winked back.

We picked up our glasses and left the table.

'Oh wait,' she said.

'What?'

'A little girl time,' she said and pointed towards the washroom.

'Cool. I will order everything necessary.'

'Fine!' she said and walked away.

I flipped open the menu in the room and ordered everything that caught my fancy! To go with it, I ordered a *lot* of alcohol! The order was there before even Malini could relieve herself. Now, the thirty thousand that they were charging for a single night seemed justified!

As I waited for Malini to come back, I could not help but think about Kabir and Avantika. Kabir had not talked to her ever since that day. I could not shake this statement off my head.

Who was Avantika talking to? I wondered if she was still waiting for me. But she had even stopped calling me. Kabir didn't even know that Avantika and I had broken up. What was Avantika up to?

These words troubled my head and I drank directly from the wine bottle. *Why? Why?*

I kept asking these questions. I kept drinking to drown the

questions out. Slowly, things had started to blur a little. I wanted them to.

'Seems like you have ordered everything there was on the menu!' Malini said as she entered the room and saw the room stacked with food and alcohol.

'Couldn't help it!' I smiled.

'Are you already drunk?' she sounded a little miffed.

'Just a little bit,' I said, though my eyes were rolling over. 'Come! Let's have shots!'

She did so and I really felt like kissing her then. Or maybe it was just the alcohol. She looked fabulous. The little girl time in the washroom had paid off. Or the alcohol had.

The Truman Show. The movie started and we started snuggling up to each other. Shots after shots found their way down our throats! I was totally getting wasted.

'You shouldn't have drunk so much,' she laughed out.

'Why?'

'We wouldn't be able to make love now! You will sleep half way . . .'

'Ah . . . you challenge me?'

'I sure do, Deb.'

I grabbed her and threw her over on the couch.

'You still have time to take that back,' I said as I ran my hands over her legs while pinning her down by her hand. She looked at me in defiance. Her eyes mocked me as she smiled wickedly.

'I won't,' she said, her lips curved as if to shoo me away. I leaned forward to kiss her and fell wayward on the floor. Head first. Luckily, I was drunk, so it did not hurt a bit.

We both laughed out.

'Okay . . . now that is a miss,' I said and she smiled.

'You are such a girl. And I don't make out with girls . . .'

'I want to make out with a girl! And you make me so lusty! We sooo need to make out . . .' I shouted out. I was clearly drunk!

'We aren't making out! You are getting your *girl* back,' she said.

'I am not getting anyone back! You are my girl!' I stood tall and shouted out, obviously shaking in my shoes. I was totally sloshed.

'Is it?'

'Yes, Malini! You are my girlfriend now . . . and I make that announcement, right *NOW!*'

'Are you sure, Deb?'

'Sure, AS I HAVE . . . As I have never been before,' I shouted.

'Is it?'

'Yes! Can we make out now? Can we make out now . . . just to seal the deal? Can we make out . . .' I grabbed her.

'Nah . . . we aren't making out! Neither did they . . .' she said breaking out of my embrace.

'*They?*'

'Kabir and Avantika . . .'

'YES! They didn't need to make out! They didn't have to make out out! I agree!' I shouted again. Everything had started to get confusing. Words were not registering in my head.

'And they didn't! *THEY DIDN'T MAKE OUT!*'

'What? They didn't!? They did!' I said. Alcohol makes your brain cells dead.

'They didn't make out,' she said sternly.

'Yes. They made out! Avantika told me!'

'I just talked to Kabir. They didn't even kiss,' she said.

For a brief moment, I was back to my senses, and then everything blacked out.

I passed out. *Darkness. They didn't make out?*

If I Would Have Known

I woke up next morning with a terrible headache. My head was pounding. My throat had dried up and my lips were parched. I felt terrible.

'Let's go,' Malini said. 'It's twelve.' She was shaking me from head to toe.

'Huh? Oh . . . right.'

Fuck! Flight!

We left that place and took the resort pick up back to the flat. I slept all the way through. My head still hurt and it only became a little better when she made lime juice for me.

'You still drink like a girl,' she smiled. She did not say much that day. It was understandable. I had to leave that day. I saw those packed bags all around me and it even depressed me. I would always miss these months.

'Hmm.'

I was still a little groggy. Everything was still a blur in my head. I put my head on the table and tried to get some more sleep.

'You know what to do now,' Malini said.

'What?'

I did not know what she was talking about until I gave it another thought. Alcohol makes you forget quite a lot of things, but it was not one of them. It was not something I would forget. But I have to admit, it had slipped out of my mind.

'They didn't make out.'

'Malini?' I asked and interrupted her while she was packing. There was nothing more to pack. She just didn't want to look at me that day. She had tears in her eyes.

'Yes?' She asked.

'You were kidding last night, right?'

'Kidding? About what?'

'Kabir and Avantika? They made out, right?'

'No, why would I? I wasn't lying,' she said, her voice was serious and cold. She was *not* messing around.

'Maybe Kabir lied. He is a bastard, right?'

'Is it? You think he *is* a bastard?'

'Yes, why! Don't you?' I asked.

'If he was a bastard, he would have told me that he had made out! He would have said that he was still doing so!' said Malini and got back to packing my bags.

'Then?' I asked.

My mind had stopped processing anything. Nothing made sense. Was Malini lying? Was Kabir lying? Was Avantika lying? *Why* would any one of them lie?

There was someone who was lying here, right?

'Is too hard for you to get, Deb?'

'What *is* there to get? Kabir lied, that's it!' I said.

'Kabir didn't lie. Avantika did! She *lied*,' she said and looked away.

'Avantika?'

'Yes, your girlfriend *lied* to you! Don't you get it?'

'But why?'

'She was *your* girlfriend. Figure it out.'

'Did she want to get rid of me?' I asked. Obviously, she did not. Why would she? I was everything to her. Avantika did everything to get back with me. But why would she do it? Why would she lie?

'No, Einstein,' she said, 'she did *not* want to get rid of you.'

'Will you *stop* being so sarcastic?'

'Then, what do you want me to act like? Like your girlfriend?' She snapped.

'Why are you snapping at me like that?' I asked. She did not say anything. I sipped on my lime juice and my head was hurting more than before.

'Deb, I am sorry. I am just a little ticked off. I will be okay. But isn't this great? She did *not* cheat on you! That is what matters. Whatever her reasons maybe, she didn't leave you. She never wanted to. It's you who left her!'

'I did *not* leave her. She did. She made out! She made me leave her,' I defended.

'She didn't! She lied. Don't be so dumb,' she said.

'What?'

'Yes, at least it makes a few things clear! You should go and get her; she probably is still waiting for you to realize how much she loved you. Maybe, she is still waiting for you to tell her how much you love *me*,' she paused and realized the mistake,' . . . I mean how much you love *her*. Go, run back to her, go back to her, this is a sign, don't you think so?'

'I don't think so,' I said. 'Why would she lie?'

'Maybe, she just wanted to test you,' she said.

I did not know what to say. Lie? Who would lie about such

a thing? Was she testing me? Who would test anyone like that? But if she was testing me, I had failed. I had left her just because she told me that she made out with someone.

She used to message that the relationship meant everything to her! Then, why did she have to lie and finish it? Why did she want to test it? *Why* the hell would Avantika do so? What the fuck did I do?

I just wished in those moments that I had not met Kabir.

'I can't go back to her,' I said.

'Would you be able to live with the fact that you broke up for something she never did?' she said.

'But she told me she *did* it.'

'And you broke up. That's what she wanted to check!' she said.

'*Why* would she do that? She knew I loved her,' I said.

'Loved her? That's why you broke up with her so easily?' she asked.

'Umm . . . But why did she do it?' My eyes had welled up.

'It does not matter what *she* did . . . what matters is what *you* do now.'

My world just turned upside down. The last few months, I had been blaming Avantika for wrecking my life. But it was a lie! I was the wrong one. I sat back and my head clouded with thoughts of Avantika and what I had done.

Though I had been utterly selfish all these years, in those moments, I really felt I should *not* be with Avantika. Why does she always have to be right? Why does she always have to be prefect? Why couldn't Avantika could have just gone out with Kabir and slept with him? Why did she have to test me?

She had made me feel like an asshole. I left her because Kabir had kissed her. Was is all that mattered to me. She made me realize that my love for her wasn't strong.

But, why did she have to stop calling me once she went to Mumbai? Maybe, she had given up. She had lost all hope that I would go back to her.

And Malini?

Suddenly, my relationship with Malini was based on a lie that Avantika told me. I would rather be alone than to be unfair to her. If I were to leave Malini and go back to Avantika, what would it do to Malini? It would be hard for her. She would have nobody.

Why did *I* have to screw up everything? Why did I have to hurt *everyone* who ever loved me?

'I am doing nothing. I do not deserve her. I have done enough to screw her life up and I am not doing the same again. I mean, I cheated, I left her when she said she did, when she actually didn't! How will I explain this? I lived with you all these months.

I have hurt her enough. She doesn't need to be with me. She is better off alone. I am better off alone. At least I will not end up hurting someone.'

'Don't be stupid. You should be with her,' she said and her voice cracked up.

'And you?' I walked up to her.

'I will be fine. I always have been, Deb.'

'I don't want to leave you,' I said and I hugged her.

'You have to. You probably don't want to right now, but you will not regret it. She is your life,' she said. She had tears in her eyes.

'I don't want *this* to go waste. I don't want us to go waste. I want to stay.'

'I want you to stay too, but it can't be. You can*not* change it! And don't worry, I will find someone. Someone better than *you*!'

'You will?'

'I will never look for one . . .' She clung to me and burst out in tears. We stood there like that for quite some time before the bell rang. It was the taxi. I felt sorry for her. I should have been happy about Avantika and Kabir, but I was more sad for Malini.

'Won't you see me off at the airport?'

'I can't see you go,' she let go off me.

'Won't you wave at me?'

'I will wave at every plane that goes over this afternoon. Wave back,' she said with tears in her eyes.

'I will miss you,' I said.

'I will miss you too,' she said.

We kissed for a few brief moments. We were not drunk this time. It felt good. I opened the door and the driver loaded the luggage on to the lift.

'I have to go now.'

'Yes. Be safe. Careful with your things. And take care. Do eat on time,' she said.

'I will.'

'Bye,' she said.

'Bye. Take care of yourself.'

'Hmm . . .'

As I turned around to leave her house, I heard her whisper to herself, *'Love you.'*

I paused for a few moments outside the door. Everything from the first day I had stepped inside that flat to this moment when I was leaving the place flashed in front of me. I wanted to hug her again for one last time. But the taxi honked. I had to leave. I promised myself, that I would come back for more.

As the taxi left the complex, I looked at the balcony where Malini and I used to spend our Fridays with a coffee and each other. She was not there. My phone beeped. It was a message from Malini. The message seemed familiar.

Her message read:

> *Sorry to have looked into your cell phone. But then we had nothing to hide from each other. And this seemed appropriate.*
>
> *If I'd only known . . .*
> *That this is the last time we've met,*
> *I would have stopped the break of dawn.*
> *And stopped the sun to set . . .*
>
> *If I'd only known*
> *That I would not ever see you again,*
> *I would have framed a picture of you within,*
> *To end my suffering, to end my pain.*
>
> *If I'd only known,*
> *That this is d last time I sit by your side,*
> *I would have told u how much I loved you,*
> *Keeping rest things aside.*
>
> *If I'd only known,*
> *That we would never hold hands again,*

I would have held them strong,
N never let anything go wrong.

If I'd only known,
That you would stand always by my side,
I would have fought d world for you,
Breaking all d walls through,

If I'd only known,
That your love was true,
If I'd only known that you would come back soon,
I would have waited for you to come by,

If I'd only known any of this,
That you were what I was breathing for,
I would have breathed my last for you,
Seen you enough and bid you adieu,
While all I can do now,
Is sit here . . .
*   . . . and wait.*

Love you.
If I'd only known. Bye Deb.
Malini.

My heart pounded, my brain felt heavy, and my eyes welled up. I tried not to think what she would be doing. She would be crying. I wanted to rush back above, hug her, and do something about it. *Anything*. I wanted to tell her that I didn't deserve her. Or anyone else. Her. Avantika. No one.

Malini. She screwed me, and then saved me and I gave her nothing.

The car drove into the airport and the driver loaded my luggage into the trolley. I felt emptiness inside me. I looked at my cell phone. I wished Malini would call. But she didn't. She once told me that she would never call or message once I leave for Bangalore. She told me that it had to end someday, and this is how she would end it. She will be out of sight and out of mind. I had always thought she was kidding. Probably she was not.

I collected my boarding pass and headed for the waiting area. A lot of flights were being cancelled those days due to bad weather, so Malini had asked to me check for mine before leaving. I had not. I sat there thinking about her. And Avantika. She lied and I failed her. Just as I had failed Malini. I finished everything.

Avantika would not take me back, why would she, had I loved her, I wouldn't have left her.

Maybe, I should just stay alone for a while, I thought to myself. I glanced up to see the flight schedule. Two flights stood out. A flight to Bangalore meant a new life. The flight to Mumbai meant the old one—Avantika!

| Bangalore. | MDLR Airlines. | 2:00 pm | Cancelled |
| Mumbai | Indigo | 2:15pm | Delayed |

I stood there staring at the flight chart. Bangalore - *Cancelled*. *Bangalore - Cancelled*.

I kept looking the board. Malini has asked to call her once I boarded the flight. There was no flight now. My eyes kept shifting from Bangalore . . . .to Mumbai . . . Mumbai.

Should I tell Malini about the flight? Or catch the next flight to Bangalore? Or should I get on the flight to Mumbai?

I flipped open my cell phone and dialled a number. I was being an asshole again. We are allowed one big mistake in our lives, aren't we? I was being selfish again. I was being Deb again. I was being spineless again. I dialled the number. The phone rang.

'Hey . . .' the voice said from the other side.

'Hi Avantika . . .'

I looked up the flight schedule board. The words, the letter, the numbers . . . everything became clearer!

Mumbai	Indigo	2:15pm	Delayed

The Short Phone Call!

I chose my old life.

'Where are you?' Avantika asked.

'. . . minutes away from a flight to Bangalore,' I said. I wanted to get out of the phone and hug her. I wanted to kiss her and make her mine again.

'Oh, new job. Best of luck,' she said. It was such a pleasure to hear her again. I almost had an erection. How could I not be with her!

'Thank you, Avantika,' I said.

'So when's your flight?'

'I am thinking of missing my flight,' I said. I had not decided what I would say when I made that call. But as I talked to her, it became clearer.

'What? Why?' she asked.

'. . . I am coming to Mumbai,' I said.

'Mumbai? *Why?*' she sounded genuinely shocked.

'I met Kabir,' I said, 'I know you lied.'

'Umm.' Now, she had nothing to say.

'I know you love me,' I said, ' . . . and I love you.'

'What if you hadn't met Kabir?'

'Sooner or later, I would have run back to you!' I said. She was not convinced by what I had said.

'Sooner? It's been three months, Deb,' she said and her voice started to crack.

'The next flight to Mumbai leaves in an hour. I should get a ticket! I said.

'But—'

'We will talk when I get there!' I said.

She was still talking when I cut the phone. She didn't want me to come, but I didn't care anymore. I looked at the girl at the tickets counter and she smiled and said, 'One ticket to Mumbai?'

'Yes please!'

I took the ticket and walked away from the counter. The ticket counter girl shouted from behind, *'Go! Get her!'*

Epilogue

Yes, I went to Mumbai. Well, it had been two months that I had been in Mumbai. No job. No place to stay. No money. But I had only one thing on my mind. Avantika.

Avantika had been playing hard to get. She said I didn't love her as much as she loved me. She had been making me run after her!

I knew she hated me for leaving her and for failing her test, but I knew she would give it up and come back to me! She knew we had to be together. I loved her and she loved me. Nothing would change that.

It was just a matter of time before she would be in my arms again! She just wanted to be sure that I wouldn't leave her again.

Malini, on the other hand, went back to Canada.

Yes, she said she'd realized how hard it would be to live in the same place that she and I had shared. She had called me up a few times and had realized that it was a lost cause. And she didn't want to come between the two of us. I had tried hard to make Malini stay in Delhi, but she hadn't. One fine day, she had left.

'I will always think of you,' said Malini. This was the last thing she had said to me.

I wished I could tell her the same. She was one of the best things to have happened to me. *Ever.*

Oh, yes, Mittal had found himself a girl. And he is losing weight again. He says he would get a six pack in the next two months. He said he's in love again. I am happy for him!

Shashank got engaged to Geetika! *Yay!* Hats off to that guy! He managed to pull it off. We all thought it was a lost battle but apparently it was not. They were getting married in three months. I was happy for them. In my free time, I wished my story would go like his too!

So, yes, I am still waiting for Avantika to come back to me! I am sure she will. It's just a matter of time. And when she comes, she will be the happiest girl in the whole wide world!

And this time . . . I swear—I won't be kissing anyone else!